Caught in the Crossfire

Slocum crossed the dusty, wagon-rutted street, heading toward the smell of horses and sweat and manure. That's when he saw it—a quick flash, a glimmer, a brief streak of silver light. But it was enough to send a shiver of shock through him. He ducked, his right hand flying to the butt of his big Colt .44, and whirled to present a thinner target.

A split second later, he made out the crack of a rifle, saw the puff of white smoke, then heard the whine of a bullet as it sizzled past him, just over his head.

The shooter was good, Slocum thought, as he cocked his single-action revolver again. Still racing toward the shooter, he caught another movement from the corner of his eye, and when he swung his head to look, he saw another rifle snout emerge from behind the main building.

In another second, he knew, he would be caught in a crossfire, out in the open, with no place to hide.

D1569986

JAKE LOGAN

SLOCUM
AND THE LADY IN BLACK

JOVE BOOKS, NEW YORK

This is a work of fiction. Names, characters, places, and incidents either
are the product of the author's imagination or are used fictitiously,
and any resemblance to actual persons, living or dead, business
establishments, events, or locales is entirely coincidental.

SLOCUM AND THE LADY IN BLACK

A Jove Book / published by arrangement with
the author

PRINTING HISTORY
Jove edition / August 2002

Copyright © 2002 by Penguin Putnam Inc.

Visit our website at
www.penguinputnam.com

ISBN: 0-515-13350-7

A JOVE BOOK®
Jove Books are published by The Berkley Publishing Group,
a division of Penguin Putnam Inc.,
375 Hudson Street, New York, New York 10014.
JOVE and the "J" design
are trademarks belonging to Penguin Putnam Inc.

PRINTED IN THE UNITED STATES OF AMERICA

10 9 8 7 6 5 4 3 2 1

1

John Slocum could hardly believe the advertisement he was reading in the Springfield *News-Journal*. He would have thought it was a mistake, except that he had seen a flyer with much the same information the night before when he had put up his horse at the livery next door.

The ad read:

FOR SALE. Tennessee-bred horses. Morgan-Arabian blood, sound of limb and teeth. 4–5 years old. $30 a head to the right person.

There had to be a catch, he thought. The rest of the ad gave the location, the same as that on the flyer he had seen the night before:

See at Collins freight yard, 4 pm, Saturday only, Commerce and Elm Streets.

He noted that the freight yard was not far from the hotel. He could probably walk there.

Slocum was intrigued by the advertisement as he sat drinking his coffee, and smoking a cigar at his table in the dining room of the Mayfair Hotel on Commerce Street in Springfield, Missouri. He had arrived the night before after riding in from Kansas City. His horse had gone lame after stepping in a rut or a gopher hole about two miles from town. He had walked the big Appaloosa in the rest of the way.

Ernie Begley, the man at the livery, which was right next to the hotel, had thought the horse's ankle might be broken. He said he'd let Slocum know for sure later on this morning. Slocum didn't think the ankle was broken, but it was badly swollen and he was worried about it.

Slocum had gotten in late, gotten a room in the hotel, drunk some Kentucky bourbon, then eaten supper after the dining room had been closed. He'd had cold leftovers, and had been glad to get them at that late hour. He had gone to bed bone-tired, his feet sore from walking in boots those last two miles.

He was supposed to meet the liveryman and the veterinarian this morning at ten o'clock. It was only seven o'clock according to the big Waterbury over the lobby entrance.

Slocum looked up and saw that other patrons were reading the same edition of the newspaper, which was not surprising, since the paperboy had been by earlier with a sheaf of papers under his arm, hawking them for a nickel apiece.

Slocum had noticed the comely young woman sitting at a table by the front window when he had entered the dining room. She had noticed him too, and throughout his breakfast she had been stealing glances his way. Whenever he looked at her, though, she turned her head away and looked out the window, or off in the distance. She didn't look like a hotel lady. She was primly dressed and had an air of refinement about her. She too was drinking coffee, having finished her slight breakfast of toast and peaches.

The waiter passed by, and Slocum beckoned for him to come to his table. The waiter changed course and stopped at Slocum's table, his eyebrows lifted in a questioning stare.

"Sir?"

"Wonder if I might borrow your pencil for a moment?" Slocum asked.

"Yes, sir." The waiter handed Slocum his stub of a pencil, then looked over his shoulder as Slocum circled the advertisement for the horses.

"Interested in horses, sir?" the waiter asked.

"That's why I came to Springfield," Slocum said. "Know anything about these offered for sale?"

"No, sir. I don't know nothin' about horses."

Slocum handed the pencil back to the waiter. The waiter left, and was hailed by another man sitting in the back corner near the lobby entrance. Slocum had noticed him before because he too had been glancing his way whenever he thought Slocum wasn't looking. But Slocum noticed such things out of long habit. He had made note of all the diners when he had entered the room, and the girl at the window and the man at the back table had both shown more than an ordinary interest in him. The other diners ate with their faces buried in their plates, and seemed intent on getting the meal over with and leaving before the sun got any higher in the spring sky.

Slocum couldn't hear what the waiter was saying to the man in the corner, but the waiter was looking in Slocum's direction and nodding. Slocum noticed too that the woman was looking over in his direction, a look of mild curiosity on her face.

After the waiter left the back table and tended another table that was empty, the woman got up from her table and walked over to Slocum's. She was carrying her copy of the paper, and it was opened to the classified advertisements just as Slocum's was.

She looked down at Slocum's paper and smiled wanly. She had pretty hair, slightly dark and shining as if she had just washed it. Ringlets fell down next to her cheeks. She had pretty green eyes, and wore a touch of rouge on her cheeks and lips, just enough to give them some color. She certainly was no painted lady, Slocum thought.

She wore a simple dress with a high bodice, and there was no jewelry around her neck or on her wrists. She carried a small change purse with a gold clasp. Her long dress failed to hide her shapely figure, and Slocum knew that her legs were slim, and probably her ankles as well.

"I notice that you circled that advertisement in the paper," she said.

"What advertisement was that?" Slocum asked.

"The one offering some fine-bred horses for a low price."

"I may have. What's your interest?"

"What's yours?" she asked, and by her bold tone, Slocum knew that beneath that refined air, this lady had some spunk in her. "Are you interested in buying fine horseflesh?" she added.

"I'm always interested in fine horseflesh," Slocum said, scanning her up and down with his piercing blue-eyed gaze.

"May I sit down?" she asked.

Slocum waved her to a chair, but did not rise to pull it out for her. Nor did she seem to expect it, he noticed. Instead, she sat down, placed her change purse on the table next to her, and looked him straight in the eye.

"I'm Margaret Collins," she said. "My friends call me Meg. And you?"

"I'm John Slocum."

"Hmm. A nice hard name. It suits you."

"I hope so. I've had it a long time."

"I mean John is such a stalwart name. And Slocum bespeaks of the salt of the earth. Not a common name, but one with the sound of a blacksmith's hammer in it. I like your name."

"Meg is a pretty name too," Slocum said, still wondering why she had come over to his table.

"It's ugly," she said. "And Margaret's not much better. Only longer. But that advertisement you circled was placed by my sister, Linda Collins. Now,

Linda is a pretty name and, in Spanish, the word means beautiful."

"And is she?" Slocum asked.

"Oh, yes, very," Meg replied.

"So are you."

Meg blushed, and Slocum noted that the color in her cheeks made her even more fascinating, and beautiful. There was something about a woman blushing that put fire in his loins, something that made a woman even more desirable.

"Why, thank you, Mr. Slocum." She patted her cheeks as if to douse the color, but the blush remained, like a rosy flower on her face. "I'm to meet Linda at noon. I rode in from Rogersville late last night after getting word that our father had died. I was too tired to go any farther. The funeral's at twelve-thirty in the Methodist church. I wonder if you would like to accompany me."

"Is that why you came over to my table?"

"No. I came to warn you about that man sitting back in the corner who's been watching you."

"I noticed him. Who is he?"

She leaned over then, keeping her voice low so that it wouldn't carry to that back table.

"His name is Pete Ferguson," she said. "He works for Karl Tolliver."

"Those names don't mean anything to me," Slocum said.

"The Tolliver brothers, Karl and Ivan, own a freight company here in Springfield. They're in competition with my fath—with my sister."

"They say competition's good for business."

"Not in this case. Ferguson there is nothing more than an outlaw. Karl uses him to scare people, and it's been said that Ferguson has killed several men."

"Any proof?"

Meg shook her head, made a wry face. "No, but he's got blood on his hands. I'd bet money on it."

"Are you a betting lady?" Slocum asked.

"It's just an expression. Look at him. He looks like a killer. Like a murderer."

Slocum did not turn around. He knew there was no way to tell what was in a man's heart by the look on his face. To him, Ferguson looked like a banker, or a drummer. Like any average citizen. But Slocum was interested in what Meg had to say. After all, the man had been looking at him with more curiosity than was necessary.

"I'll watch my back," Slocum said.

"Uh-oh," Meg said suddenly. "He's getting up. I think he's coming over here."

Slocum did not turn around, but he slid one hand off the table and let it dangle near the butt of his big Colt .44 on his right hip. He carried a concealed belly-gun inside his shirt, tucked behind his belt, and his hand was not far from that weapon either.

Out of the corner of his eye, Slocum saw the man leave his table and walk toward them. The stranger wore a suit coat, so Slocum could not tell right away if the man was packing iron, but he would know in a minute, he was sure.

"Miss Collins," Ferguson said as he reached the table.

Meg nodded, but did not say anything.

"Mr. Slocum. I'm Pete Ferguson. I hear you're in town to buy some horses."

"Where'd you hear that?" Slocum asked.

"From Ernie Begley, the liveryman."

"Yes, I did tell him that last night."

"Some advice for you, Slocum. If you want to buy horses here in Springfield, come on out to the Tolliver freight yards. Just ride right up on Glenstone, until you come to Battlefield Road. You'll find us."

"Thanks," Slocum said. "I'll keep that in mind. I haven't had a chance to look at any stock yet."

"Just make sure you don't buy none from Collins Freight. You might make a bad deal there."

"That sounds like a threat to me, Ferguson."

"Take it any way you want. Miss Collins."

Pete Ferguson touched the brim of his hat and turned on his heel. In a moment he was gone from the dining room.

Slocum took a puff from his cigar. Meg fanned the smoke away as he exhaled a blue plume into the air. "I'm sorry," Slocum said. "Does the smoke bother you?"

"No, I like the smell of cigars. My daddy smoked."

Slocum took another puff and stubbed the cigar out on his plate. He glanced at the lobby through the entrance. It was empty.

"Are you finished with your coffee, Mr. Slocum?"

"Yes. I'm going up to my room."

"So am I. Would you be so kind as to accompany me? I have to change for the funeral, but I'd like to talk to you some more. In private."

"All right."

"Then you'll accompany me to the funeral? You can meet my sister and then we can all have lunch and go to the freight yards where you can look over the horses she has for sale."

"Apparently that feller that was here doesn't want me to buy any horses from your sister."

"Can we discuss this in my room, Mr. Slocum? I do want to freshen up."

"All right," Slocum said. He left some bills on the table, and took Meg's arm and walked to the lobby. A young man approached him.

"I shined your boots, Mr. Slocum, and cleaned your frock coat. I left them in your room."

"Thanks," Slocum said. He pressed a coin into the young man's hand.

"Thank you, sir."

Slocum headed for the stairs, with Meg on his arm. Just then he saw Ferguson emerge from a dark corner of the lobby. The man headed for the front door, then stopped and turned to Slocum. "Remember what I told you, Slocum. It can be mighty risky buying horses from the wrong people."

"Ferguson," Slocum said, "as a horse drummer, you'd make a pretty good field hand. I'll buy my horses where I please. And you can tell your boss that."

"You may be sorry you said that, Slocum."

"Don't press me, Ferguson. There's a lady present, but I never was one to mind my manners."

Ferguson stomped off and went out the door. Meg gave Slocum's arm a gentle squeeze.

"You'd better watch yourself, Mr. Slocum. That man's dangerous."

"So far, all I've seen that's dangerous about him is his big mouth."

Meg laughed as they started up the stairs to her room.

2

Meg's room was two doors down from Slocum's and on the opposite side of the hall. She handed her key to Slocum and he opened the door for her, handing the key back. After they stepped inside, she turned and locked the door. The room reeked of perfume, and a single shaft of light beamed through the window. Her bed was smoothed over, but it looked slept in.

"Make yourself at home," she said. "Take a chair at that table. I just want to get out of these shoes."

She sat on the bed and took her shoes off. Then she walked over to the table and sat down in the other chair.

"Mr. Slocum," she said, "are you a gunfighter?"

"No."

"You didn't back down to Karl Tolliver's hired gunfighter. You weren't afraid of him."

"No, I wasn't afraid of him. But I wouldn't turn my back on him either."

11

"If he pulled his gun on you, would you shoot him?"

"What do you think?"

"I think you'd kill him before he killed you."

Slocum smiled, but said nothing.

"I think I've sized you up pretty well, Mr. Slocum."

"Where is all this leading, Miss Collins?"

"I'm sure my sister will explain everything to you, if you're the kind of man I think you are. I—it's just that I want to help her, if I can. She'll tell you why she put that advertisement in the paper, and if you're the man she's looking for, she'll tell you everything you need to know."

"You make such a mystery out of it. She's just selling some horses off cheap, isn't she?"

"That's not the whole of it," Meg said. She leaned over the table so she was closer to Slocum. "It has to do with our father's death, which is mainly why I'm here in Springfield. I live in Rogersville, a few miles out of town. I'm a nanny for two small children. Our mother died several years ago, and our father and Linda have been running the freight business. They couldn't afford to take care of me, so I'm on my own."

"I see," Slocum said.

"I'm a very lonely woman, Mr. Slocum. The ranch where I live is very isolated and I seldom get into town. There are no eligible men where I live."

"That must be hard on you," Slocum said. "You're young and you're blessed with beauty."

"You don't know how much your words mean to

me," she said, reaching her hand across the table to rest atop his. "When I'm out there taking care of those children all day and night, I feel like an old hag. An old, forgotten hag."

"You shouldn't, Miss Collins."

"Please call me Meg, will you?"

"If you'll call me John."

"Yes, John." She squeezed his hand, and Slocum felt the heat rising in his loins. Meg was a very attractive woman, and he was conscious that they were both alone in her hotel room. And they were very close, sitting there at the table.

"I hope you don't think I'm too forward," she said. "But you look like a man of experience."

"No, I don't think you're too forward, Meg. And I don't know what you mean by 'experience'."

"I mean, should a woman, if she desired you, ask you to take her to bed, you'd know what to do."

"I reckon that's so," he said.

"And you wouldn't think badly of such a woman afterwards, would you?"

"No, I wouldn't think badly of such a woman. If she were to ask, I would take it as a compliment. I know what lonely is, Meg, same as you."

"Yes, I expect you do, riding long distances by yourself, traveling as you do."

"Yes'm, that's so. I've just come down from Kansas City and I didn't stop at any towns along the way."

"I don't have to get dressed for some time. How about you, John?"

"I've got to see about my horse around ten."

"So, we have plenty of time, don't we?"

"For what?" Slocum asked, although he had a pretty good idea.

"To get really acquainted. We're two grown-up people. We're all alone, and I have a fairly comfortable bed there just waiting for us."

Slocum swallowed.

Before he could say anything, Meg got up from the table, walked around behind him, and leaned over. She embraced him and started pecking him on the neck. Then she nibbled an earlobe, and ran both hands down his shirt and began massaging his chest. He could smell her perfume and sense the heat of her as she rubbed her breasts against the back of his neck.

He could feel her nipples harden beneath her blouse. He turned his head and looked up at her. "Maybe we ought to do this over on that bed," Slocum said. "Without our clothes on."

"Umm, yes, that would be nice, John."

She removed her hands from inside his shirt and leaned back. Slocum arose from his chair and she was waiting for him, her lips pushed out, her breasts heaving with her short panting breaths. He kissed her and felt her melt in his arms. She pressed her breasts hard against his chest, and the nipples were still hard as acorns.

"Yes," she breathed. "Take me to bed, John. I want you."

"I want you too," he husked, and he led her toward the bed. He began to undress her, and she moved his hands away.

"Let me do it," she said. "It'll be a lot faster. And you can take off those trousers and that shirt."

He sat on the edge of the bed and removed his boots, then stripped out of his shirt and trousers as he watched her dress slide from her shoulders and drop to a puddle on the floor. She slid her undergarments off with deft movements and took the wrapping from her breasts. They plunged into view with a bounce. They looked like plump melons ripe for the picking, and the nipples stood out in rigid relief from the dark aureoles.

She flung herself atop Slocum, fully naked, and he fell back on the bed. She peppered him with kisses and groped for his manhood with her left hand, grasping it firmly with her delicate fingers.

She slid her tongue into his mouth, and Slocum turned her over and pulled her all the way onto the bed. He lay beside her, cupping her thatch with his bold hand, and she rose against it as she pushed her hips upward. She placed her mouth on his and smothered him with a long, deep kiss.

"I'm on fire," she said, breaking the kiss. She pulled on his rigid member, pumping her hand up and down its length. He could feel the light touch of her fingernails on the skin. He was fully ready for her, and as he plied her wetness with his finger, he knew she was ready too.

"Take me, John," she said, and spread her legs wide.

Slocum scooted over and mounted her as she released her hold on his prick. He looked down into her coffee-brown eyes and lowered his loins until his cock touched the portals of her womanhood. Then he entered her, and she gasped with pleasure as he sank deep into the steaming moist cavern of her cunt.

Meg more than matched Slocum hump for hump, and they soon had the bed slats creaking to a fare-thee-well. He drove in hard and deep, and she met every thrust with one of her own. She gasped and sighed as her body shook with pleasure. Her fingernails grazed his back and left long white streaks as her hands roamed up and down on either side of his spine.

"Yes, yes," she screamed softly into his ear. "That's the best I've ever had. Keep doing it."

Slocum was more than happy to oblige, and the entire bed quaked with their exuberant thrashing. He held himself as long as he could, extending her pleasure and his, until her body was sleek with sweat, her breasts glistening like dew-kissed muskmelons.

Then, with a vigorous finish, Slocum romped her to a high climax and his balls exploded with volcanic intensity. She cried out loudly, and her entire body shuddered as if she were gripped with a sudden spasm. She held him tightly as he finished gushing inside her, and held him inside her until she was satisfied that he had no more to give her.

"That was wonderful," she whispered as Slocum slid from her sweat-soaked body and lay beside her.

"You are a vigorous woman, Meg."

"And you're more than I expected, more than I ever wished for, John. You have made me a happy woman."

"Even though you're a grieving woman?"

"Yes, I'm sad about my father, but I don't want to think about that now. I'm still glowing inside."

"And outside too," he said, noticing the bloom on her cheeks, her neck, chest, and breasts. It was as if she had been covered with pale rose petals and they had melted into her skin.

She looked down at her glistening body and rubbed her hands over her chest and breasts. "Oh, my, and I just took a bath this morning."

"I had one last night," Slocum said. "It'll be a hot day and by noon, you'll be sweating anyway. I wouldn't worry about it."

"But your smell is all over me."

"And yours all over me," he said, smiling.

"That was very gallant of you, John. But time is fleeting. A woman must take care of herself and she is expected to smell nice. Especially at a funeral."

"I was just leaving," he said with a grin. "Thank you again, Meg. You're quite a woman."

"You said that, but I don't mind hearing it. Will you come back to the hotel after you see about your horse? Or should I stop by the livery and pick you up?"

"If you don't mind, you can pick me up at the livery. I may not stay another night in Springfield."

"Oh, why? It isn't because of me, I hope."

"No, I came to buy some horses. There's no hurry, but I don't get paid until I deliver them in Kansas City."

"I see. Well, I hope you do stay. At least another night."

"I'll see," Slocum said.

He arose from the bed and put his clothes back on.

"I see you carry a knife in your boot," she said. "And that's a cute little pistol you're hiding in your pants."

"I ride through some pretty rough places," he said. "I keep the hideout gun and the knife as insurance."

"Isn't that gun you carry on your hip big enough?"

"It's big enough. Sometimes it gets in the way."

"Well, you sound like a man who's prepared for anything."

"Just about," he said as he strapped on his gunbelt and slid the leather through the buckle. He hitched it tight and bent down to pick up his hat.

"A kiss before you go?" she said.

Slocum leaned over the bed and gave Meg a kiss. Just then, there was a loud knock at the door. Slocum stood up and braced himself.

"Who is it?" Meg called out.

"A message for you, Miss Collins," someone said on the other side of the door.

"Just a minute," she said.

"Do you know who that is?" Slocum asked.

"I imagine it's the boy from downstairs. The one who told you about your coat and boots."

"It doesn't sound like him," Slocum said. "You'd better let me open the door."

"Goodness," she said. "Do you think . . . ?"

Slocum strode to the door as Meg slid under the

coverlet and pulled it up over her chest to conceal her breasts.

He turned the key in the lock. It made a loud clicking sound, metal against metal. When it was unlocked, he didn't open the door, but stood there, one hand hovering over the butt of his big Colt .44.

"Just slide the message under the door," Slocum said, stepping to one side.

"Here's your goddammed message," a deep voice boomed out.

Then two quick blasts from a pistol broke the silence. Slocum ducked as two holes appeared in the door, sending wood splinters flying.

Meg screamed.

The bullets sizzled through the air and shattered the window. Glass tinkled and crashed and the curtains rustled from the passing wind caused by the speeding bullets.

Then Meg and Slocum both heard the sound of running feet down the hall.

Slocum stepped back to the door and swung it open, pistol in hand already cocked. There was no one there. He stepped into the hall just in time to see a man turn the corner and clump down the stairs. The man was too far away to see who he was.

The pounding footsteps faded away. Slocum knew he would never be able to catch whoever had taken those shots at him. By now, the man was already on the street and probably a good half a block away.

He stepped back inside the room. He eased the

hammer of the Colt back down and slid it back into its holster.

"I think that message was for me, Meg," Slocum said. "But you'd better keep an eye out. Maybe someone wants to kill you. Just be careful."

Meg shivered in fear and covered up her head.

"I'll be at the livery," he said, stepping back into the hall and closing the door.

He hoped he was right about that gunman. That the man had meant to kill Slocum, not Meg Collins.

He didn't want to think about what it would mean to Meg if he was wrong.

3

Ernie Begley, the owner of the Springfield Livery on Commercial Street, looked up when the tall man cast his shadow over him. Begley was dipping a bucket into a grain bin when Slocum walked up on him.

"Oh, Mr. Slocum. Little early, aren't you?"

"Did you have a look at the Palouse, Ernie?"

Begley wiped his hands on his leather blacksmith's apron and walked over to where Slocum stood, framed in the light streaming in from the open back door of the stable.

"I looked at that leg real good this mornin'," Begley said. "How come you... walked in the back way?"

"Habit maybe."

"You expectin' trouble?"

"What about that leg? Or ankle?"

"It's a good thing you walked that horse in here last night."

"Is the ankle broken?"

21

Begley, a short, stocky man with one gimpy leg, his head balding like a monk's tonsure, cocked one eye and opened a mouthful of carious teeth in what amounted to a crooked smile.

"Nope. Leg ain't broke. Ankle neither. Just a sprain, but a bad one."

"You got a vet around here?"

"I'm as much a vet as you'll need, Mr. Slocum."

"You tended to the ankle then."

"I soaked it in some warm water this mornin', water what was mixed with Epsom salts. Ankle was badly swolled, all right. No hairline fracture, though. Bones are sound as a Yankee dollar."

"Let me take a look at it," Slocum said.

"It's all bandaged up, but come along. I've got your horse in the back stall, coolest place in the stables."

Slocum followed Begley to the end stall. He opened the door and went inside. He bent over as the Palouse whickered in recognition. Slocum saw that the ankle was still swollen under the loosely wrapped bandage. There was no sign of blood on the wrapping.

Slocum patted the horse on its neck as he stood up.

"I've got salve under that bandage," Begley said. "When the swelling goes down some, I'll put some liniment on it that will help with the pain." The horse limped as it turned to face the open door.

"You stay here, boy," Slocum said.

"Be at least a week," Begley said. "Maybe longer."

"I can see that. Make sure he's fed corn along with his oats, will you?"

"You want me to give him an apple now and again?"

"You could do that?"

"Be another two bits for that, four bits for the grainin' per day, and a dollar-a-day board."

"I'll pay you a week in advance."

Begley grinned and wiped a sweaty palm on his apron. "That'd be mighty fine with me, Mr. Slocum. Hard coin is scarce in these parts since the war."

Slocum paid Begley, counting out the bills and coins he kept in his pocket. He was wearing his cleaned frock coat and freshly shined boots, along with his best shirt and a string tie.

"Goin' to a funeral or something?" Begley asked as he pocketed the money.

"As a matter of fact, I am. For Ralph Collins."

"I didn't know you and Collins were friends," Begley said, something guarded in his voice.

"I never met the man," Slocum said.

"Then, how come . . . ?"

"It's a long story, Ernie."

"Was I you, I'd stay away from that Collins woman."

"Which Collins woman is that?" Slocum asked.

"Why, Linda. She's bossin' the Collins freight lines now that her pappy has passed on."

"I don't know her either."

"Do you, ah, just make a habit of goin' to funerals where you don't know nobody?"

Slocum laughed. "I'm going to see Miss Linda

this afternoon and look at some of her horses she's wanting to sell."

"Yep, but she ain't bringin' them to the funeral, is she?"

"Do you know her sister? Meg?" Slocum asked.

"I don't know neither of them. But I see Miss Linda now and again. She's boarded horses with me. Meg, she lives over to Rogersville with her no-good husband."

"Meg is married?"

"Last I heard. To some lout that ain't worth the powder to blow him to hell. Name of Jasper Tolliver."

"Is he kin to Karl Tolliver?"

"Cousin, I think. Hard to keep track. Them Tollivers is thick as fleas on a hound's back."

Slocum swallowed as if to digest that bit of information. That was not the first time a woman had lied to him, and he knew it would not be the last. So Meg was married. And to a Tolliver at that. He wondered what else she had lied to him about.

"Do you know a man named Pete Ferguson?"

"I know him," Begley said. "He works for the Tollivers."

"For the Tollivers? Or for Karl Tolliver?"

"Well, sir, Karl is the head man at Tolliver Freight. I reckon Ferguson works for him."

"Hauling freight?"

Begley let out a loud guffaw and slapped his leather apron atop his calf.

"That's funny?" Slocum said.

"Have you met Ferguson?" Begley asked.

"I met him this morning."

"Did you get a close look at his hands?"

"I did. They looked as if he washed them in milk and honey."

"That's right. That man ain't done an honest day's work in his life, unless you count gunslingin' as honest work."

"I suppose in some cases you could count it that way."

"Well, not in Ferguson's case. He don't wear no badge, that 'un. No, he's what you might call a regulator."

"A regulator?"

Begley chuckled. "Yeah, he regulates for Karl Tolliver."

"Regulates what?" Slocum asked.

"That's somethin' nobody talks about. Let's just say some people who get in Karl Tolliver's path have a way of disappearin'."

"Disappearing?" Slocum asked.

"I shouldn't be talkin' out loud about any of this."

"Ferguson warned me about buying horses from Linda Collins this morning at the hotel."

"Then I'd take that as fair warnin'," Begley said. "Like I said, Ferguson's a kind of regulator."

"He makes people disappear."

"Disappear or end up on the undertaker's table."

"Any proof?" Slocum asked.

Begley shook his head. "With all those Tollivers, Ferguson always has him an alibi. I'm surprised he gave you a warning. Others haven't been so lucky."

"Maybe he was just doing some advance regulating," Slocum said.

Begley laughed. "Well, you just watch your back and your Ps and Qs while you're at it. Where you headed now?"

"Meg Collins said she'd pick me up here at the livery sometime before noon."

"You got a long wait then."

"I think I'll skip the Collins funeral. Have you got a horse I can rent?"

"What do you aim to do?" Begley asked.

"I thought I'd ride over to Collins Freight and take a look at those horses Linda has for sale. If I don't like them, I can look someplace else."

"What about Miss Meg then?"

"Tell her I changed my mind. Now, how about that horse? And maybe you can steer me in the right direction to Collins Freight."

"You don't need a horse to get there," Begley said. "Collins Freight is on Commercial Street, about six blocks from here, seven maybe. In fact, you'll pass the undertaker's on your way. If you feel like walking, that is."

"I can walk that far—even after last night," Slocum said with a wry smile.

"Yep, I reckon you can. Give that horse of yours a few days rest and my treatment and he ought to be good as new."

"About a week, you think?"

"A week, ten days maybe. He's a strong horse. Sprains generally don't heal fast, but if I keep him bandaged and salved and linimented, he ought to come along pretty fast."

"Good enough," Slocum said. He fished out a cigar from his pocket and bit off the end. He brushed the front of his frock coat and touched a hand to his hat brim. "I'll see you sometime later, Begley. You take good care of my horse."

"I'll do that, Mr. Slocum. You watch out for Ferguson."

"I will," Slocum replied, and headed for the back door of the stable, the way he had come in. He stepped outside, then stood for a moment to light his cigar and adjust his eyes so that he could see better.

He walked a few doors down and then stepped between two buildings and headed toward Commercial Street. There were quite a few people about, mostly men with horse-drawn carts and wagons, streaming back and forth in opposite directions, some carts and wagons with names on their sides, some with no legend at all. He saw very few women, and those he saw were not well dressed, although a few had parasols and wore bonnets to keep their heads cool in the blaze of the Missouri sun.

He passed the funeral home. SIMMONS FUNERAL PARLOR, it read on the outside. There was a hearse drawn up in back and two men hooking up a pair of horses to harness. He wondered where the cemetery was.

The buildings, mostly clapboard, grew sparser as he walked further along Commercial, and the country grew more rustic. He enjoyed the cigar and nodded to others who acknowledged his presence. He kept looking over his shoulder to see if he was being followed, but he saw nothing that aroused his suspicions.

Finally, he saw the sign that read COLLINS DRAY-AGE, FREIGHT HAULED, and beneath, SPRINGFIELD TO HARRISON, ARKANSAS.

All along the street were reminders of the War Between the States, which had raged in Missouri, here in Springfield, and along the Arkansas border. Missouri had been a border state that had been under the Union flag, and he saw fields full of cannon, four-pounders and six-pounders lined up in rows behind locked fences that he could see through, weapons that still sent chills up his spine and brought back memories of battles fought on bloody fields long ago and far away. In Kansas, where Slocum had fought with Quantrill's Raiders, and at Gettysburg, where his brother Robert had lost his life.

He saw the barracks beyond the cannon, and knew they probably contained rifles, guidons, and other war paraphernalia left behind when Union troops left to return home, as he had returned to Calhoun County, Georgia, where he'd found the Reconstructionists laying waste to everything held dear by Georgians, confiscating farms, including his own, as the spoils of war.

He shook off the feelings that rose up in him as he started toward the Collins freight yards, crossing the dusty, wagon-rutted street, heading toward the smell of horses and sweat and manure.

That was when he saw it. It was only a quick

flash, a glimmer, a brief streak of silver light. But that was enough to send a shiver of shock through Slocum's senses. He ducked, and his right hand flew to the butt of his big Colt .44. He whirled to present a thinner target.

An instant later, he heard the crack of a rifle. He saw the puff of white smoke, then heard the whine of a bullet as it sizzled past him, just over his head.

He drew his pistol, cocking it before it was level with his gunbelt. He saw the quick movement of a man behind a corral post on the Collins property, another flash of light as a rifle barrel swung slightly, then came to bear on him.

Slocum squeezed off a quick shot, knowing he had little chance of hitting his target from that distance, which he judged to be at least fifty yards, perhaps more, but the pistol bucked in his hand as it exploded and shot a lead bullet through its big muzzle.

Slocum hunched over even more and dashed in a zigzag pattern toward the shooter. Just before he made his first zag, the rifle belched fire and smoke and he heard the high whine of a bullet as it left the barrel and sped in his direction. The bullet tore a furrow in the ground a few yards behind him and to his right, kicking up dust and caroming off a buried rock, only to whine off, an aimless missile.

The shooter was good, Slocum thought as he cocked the single-action revolver again. Still racing toward the shooter, Slocum caught another movement from the corner of his eye, and when he swung his head to look, he saw another rifle snout emerge from behind the main building.

In another second, he knew, he would be caught in a cross fire, out in the open, with no place to hide.

4

Slocum now faced two shooters, both trying to kill him. And both of them seemed to be crack shots. Thinking fast, Slocum made a decision. He could not hope to pin down both shooters at once, so he scrambled, still zigzagging, toward the first shooter, who had the least cover. He weaved through an imaginary course, firing his pistol, dodging bullets from the second shooter, bullets that whistled past scant inches from striking him fatally.

The first shooter started backing away and Slocum went after him, running at top speed. He cracked off a shot, then another, and saw the man freeze and stiffen for a moment, then limp toward the shelter of the freight office. Slocum swung his pistol and fired at the second shooter just as a bullet whizzed past his ear, so close it made the hairs stand up on the back of his neck.

In that instant after the last rifle shot, Slocum gained the protection of the corral at the side of the office building. He hugged one of the posts and

31

opened the gate on the cylinder of his pistol. He spun it and used the ejection rod to push out the spent rounds. Then he pushed fresh bullets into the cylinder and closed the gate.

He could not see the second shooter, and he began to edge away from that side of the corral, moving quickly from post to post until he could make a run for the office. He scrambled away from the corral and ran to an empty wagon parked just in back. He huddled against it for cover, listening for any sound of someone approaching.

When he peered around the corner of the wagon, he saw that the back of the office was deserted. There was a shed in the back, with stalls, but all were empty, and one section seemed to be a small warehouse. It had a locked door with a note tacked onto it.

Slocum stepped out, then back in. That was when he heard the sound of galloping hoofbeats. They were moving away from him. Two horses, he thought as he listened. He ran from the wagon to the other side of the shed and saw two people on horseback, riding away in a hurry, both hunched over their saddlehorns so that he could not hope to identify them.

Just to make sure he was alone, Slocum walked around the other side of the office building, his pistol cocked and ready in case the two ambushers had left behind a shooter to finish him off.

But he saw no one and returned to the warehouse, walked up, and read the note. It read:

CLOSED. DEATH IN THE FAMILY.
OPEN AT 4 P.M.

He leaned against the loading dock and holstered his pistol. He got his breath back. In the excitement, he had paid no attention to the energy he was expending, but now he felt his muscles relax. He flexed his fingers to take away the stiffness from gripping his pistol.

Slocum heard a horse whinny. The sound came from behind the storehouse and shed. His senses on full alert, he walked around to the back and saw that there was more to the building than he had thought at first. The stables on the other side extended to larger ones in the back, and there was a large corral attached. There too he saw more wagons lined up, all bearing the legend COLLINS FREIGHT CO., and beneath: SPRINGFIELD, HOLLISTER, HARRISON, ARK.

Slocum walked over to the corral and gave out a low whistle. A horse stuck its head out of the stable to peer at him. Then it trotted out, followed by another. He could see the Arabian bloodlines in the animals. They were beautiful, and he slipped inside the corral and spoke to them in soothing tones.

"Here, boy, let me take a look at you," Slocum said, grasping the first horse's jaw underneath while patting him on the neck. He leaned down and felt up and down both front legs, rubbed the chest. He pried open the horse's mouth and examined its teeth, nodding with satisfaction.

"Sound as a Yankee dollar," Slocum said to himself.

He looked the other horse over too, and liked what he saw. He spoke to both animals and then climbed back out of the corral. He walked into the barn and looked inside, squinting his eyes to adjust them to the lack of light, then opening them again when they had adjusted to the change.

The stalls were neat and clean, with fresh straw on the ground in each one, well stocked with grain and water. He was getting the idea that Collins ran a first-class operation. There were other horses inside, and they appeared to be well groomed and showed signs of having been curried that morning. He was surprised no one was about, but he supposed the hands were all getting ready for the funeral.

Slocum had seen enough. He wanted to go outside and light up a cigar. Then he planned to walk back into town and return at four o'clock that afternoon and talk horses with Miss Linda Collins.

He was about to walk outside the way he had come in when he heard a slight noise behind him. He started to turn, and felt a smashing blow to the back of his head. He knew he was in trouble for an instant after the blow was struck, but then everything started to turn black. He felt himself falling forward as his senses left him, and by the time he hit the ground, he felt no pain and fell into the deep darkness of unconsciousness.

That was the last he remembered as he swam in the depths of total oblivion.

5

Slocum felt the splash of warm water strike him in the face, bringing him back to consciousness. He tried to rise as he spluttered and gasped for breath. But his hands and feet were tied with manila rope, the type used to make lariats.

He opened his eyes and looked up. A man and a woman stood there, staring down at him. The woman looked familiar, but he could not place her. He was still addled from being struck on the head and was still trying to get his bearings.

The woman was dressed all in black, wearing a black hat with a veil pulled up so that he could see her face. She stood with her legs slightly apart, her arms akimbo. She wore very little makeup, a splash of rouge on her cheeks and a tinge of color on her full ripe lips.

The man standing next to the woman was short and stocky, dressed in a dark, ill-fitting suit that he had obviously outgrown a few years before. He was aiming a scattergun at Slocum, and there was just a trace of a gap-toothed smile on his face.

Slocum struggled with his bonds. He was tied hands and feet, with one section of rope linking the two places. He was trussed up like a Christmas turkey, and both his side arm and his belly-gun were missing.

"Who are you?" the woman asked. "And what the hell are you doing snooping around here?"

"The name's John Slocum, and I was looking over those horses for sale out there."

"Clyde here said you were here in the barn. The advertisement said four o'clock, and you were here this morning."

"I didn't have anything else to do. Ah, could you untie me, please, ma'am? These ropes are mighty uncomfortable."

"I'll bet you work for that skunk Tolliver, don't you?" she said.

"No, ma'am. I don't work for anybody except myself."

"He works for Tolliver, all right," the man next to her said. "He was sneakin' around here like somebody up to doing mischief."

"You're not from around here," the woman said.

"No. I rode in last night from Kansas City," Slocum said.

"What's your business here in Springfield?"

"I came here to buy some horses."

"And you saw my advertisement."

"Yes."

"Well, you've seen the horses I have for sale. Anything wrong with them?" she asked.

"Well, you're selling them too cheap."

The woman threw her head back and laughed. Then she slapped her thigh in a fit of mirth. "You sound like an honest man, mister. Clyde, untie Mr. Slocum."

"Miss Collins, I think—"

"Never mind, Clyde. Untie him. And put down that damned scattergun."

"Yes'm," Clyde said, and leaned the shotgun against a wooden support, leaving it within easy reach.

Clyde bent down and began untying the ropes that bound Slocum. "You watch him real careful, Miss Collins," he said. "If he jumps me, you grab up that scattergun and let him have both barrels."

"I don't think that will be necessary, Clyde," she said.

"Thank you, ma'am," Slocum said with a grin.

When Clyde had untied all the knots, he stepped back and stood next to the shotgun. Slocum got to his feet. He rubbed his wrists and patted the dust off his frock coat and trousers.

"Now, if you'd kindly give me back my pistols, Clyde, I'll feel a whole lot better."

Clyde looked at Miss Collins. "I got 'em locked up in the tack room," he said.

"Go and get them, Clyde," she said.

"Now, Mr. Slocum," she said as Clyde snatched the scattergun away from the post and carried it with him as he walked to a far corner of the stables, "tell me about yourself."

"Not much to tell really," he said.

"Do I detect a speck of Southern accent in your speech? Georgia maybe? Alabama?"

"Georgia, ma'am. I hail from Calhoun County."

"You're a long way from home," she said.

"Ma'am, home is where I'm at."

"I see. A drifter."

"I prefer the term 'traveling man.' "

"Let's go to my office. We can talk there. You interest me, Mr. Slocum."

"You can call me John if you like, ma'am."

"Well, then, I will. And you can call me Miss Collins."

Slocum's face did not change expression, but he was forming an opinion of "Miss Collins" as they walked to a door in the stable, went through it, and came out behind the front building. There was a back door, which she entered and left open for him.

The office was neat, spartan, looked efficient. There was a potbellied stove for winter, a large desk with boxes full of papers on the corners, a spindle, pen, and ink. There was a bench, two chairs. Linda Collins sat behind her desk and waved Slocum to one of the chairs in front of it.

He sat down, and she looked him over a long time before she spoke. She picked up a pencil that was new and stuck one end in her mouth. She had a very nice mouth, he thought.

"Are you an adventurous man, John?" she asked finally.

"That depends on what you mean by adventurous."

"Are you a man who takes risks? Can you put your life on the line?"

"I try not to take unnecessary risks," he said. "May I smoke? I see an ashtray on your desk. A cigar."

"A cigar? My father smoked cigars. I like a man who smokes cigars."

Slocum dug in his pocket for a cheroot. He offered her one. She shook her head. He struck a lucifer on the heel of his boot and lit the end of the cigar. He blew the smoke away from Linda Collins.

"As for putting my life on the line," he said, "that would depend on the circumstances. I will defend myself if attacked, and I've stuck my neck out for a few people who were worth it."

Clyde entered the office, carrying Slocum's pistols. He handed them to Slocum, who examined them before putting his Colt in his holster and the .32-caliber belly-gun beneath his shirt and behind his belt.

"You pack enough iron," Clyde said.

"One can't be too careful," Slocum said. "Especially if a man was to sneak up behind him."

"I was doin' my job," Clyde said.

"And you're good at it, Clyde."

"I work for Miss Collins and she pays me to protect her interests."

"Do you always attack customers who come to see Miss Collins?" Slocum asked.

"Clyde, that will be all," Collins said with an abruptness that surprised her employee. He nodded and backed away, then went out the back door.

"You didn't need to pick on Clyde that way," she said.

Slocum rubbed the back of his head. "I've got a knot back here that Clyde gave me, Miss Collins. I think he acted in haste, to be polite about it."

"He was protecting my interests."

"If he keeps doing that to your customers, you won't have many interests left."

"You have a sharp tongue, John. If your wits are half as sharp, I might have a proposition for you."

"A proposition?"

"I ran that advertisement in the newspaper to see what kind of person would show up. Those horses, as you say, are worth more than thirty dollars a head."

"And I'm the only one?"

"So far. Frankly, I didn't expect anyone to show up."

"Then why run the notice?"

Linda Collins laughed. "I wanted to see if there was one man in town who didn't pee his pants and shake in his boots at the mention of the name Tolliver."

"Tolliver?"

"My competitor in the freight-hauling business."

"This Tolliver has everyone buffaloed?"

"More than that. He's put the word out that nobody who wants to keep breathing should do any business with me, or work for me."

"Then how do you do any business?" Slocum asked.

"I have business, luckily. Merchants still need to

conduct commerce between here and Harrison, Arkansas. Tolliver can't handle it all, and he's got his own route. I have mine."

"Then what's the problem, Miss Collins?"

"My father ran this business. He built it and he hauled freight for it. He was killed a few days ago. Murdered. I've just come from his funeral. I miss him terribly already."

Slocum thought she was going to cry, but she steeled herself and fought back any sign of emotion. He gave her credit for that. This woman had some iron in her, he thought.

"I have two drivers working for me now," she continued. "Both of them are on their way to Harrison. I want to make sure they come back. We haul goods there and haul goods back. I need a man to ride down there and find out if they'll be safe on the return trip."

"And if they won't be?"

"Then I want a man who'll make sure they are safe. I suspect that Tolliver might want to waylay my drivers and either kill them or scare them off."

"You want a hired gun, in other words," Slocum said.

Collins leaned back in her chair and shot Slocum a look that he could only interpret as sizing him up even more.

"I won't descend to Tolliver's level," she said. "But Karl Tolliver has declared war on Collins Freight, and I intend to fight him with all my heart. I'm looking for a man who won't back down to him, and who can carry some authority when he runs my freight line."

"So, you want a man to go down to Arkansas and ride shotgun?"

"No. I want Tolliver to know that someone will be watching him. I want a man to make all the stops, tell the people he works for me and he's going to regulate my line."

"Regulate your line?" Slocum asked.

"Enforce the safety of my drivers and the goods we haul."

"You want some muscle then."

"I want a man with balls to ride the line and make a lot of noise."

"And shoot anyone who tries to kill one of your drivers."

"John, I'm not going to pussyfoot around the issue here. These are hard men I'm bucking, and they respect force. But at heart, they're a bunch of cowards. My father was shot in the back. He didn't deserve to die. Not like that. I'm looking for a man who has eyes in the back of his head and who isn't busy handling and hauling freight. I want a man who can find out who shot my father and either bring him to justice or put his lamp out."

"What if there's more than one man?"

"If the man I hire is outnumbered, he can count on me and my drivers to back him up."

Slocum didn't say anything. He was looking at a determined woman, a woman who meant business. There were so many holes in her plan, it looked like a giant sieve to him. But he understood her problem.

He knew what bullies were, and Karl Tolliver was stacking up to be a big bully, one who would kill off the man in the business and then try to intimidate his daughter. Slocum had run into such scoundrels before. The West was teeming with such men.

There was a large Waterbury clock on the wall. Linda glanced up at it and then back to Slocum. He looked at it too, and saw that the minute hand had slipped down to the six.

"It's four-thirty," she said. "It looks like you're the only one who wants to buy my horses cheap."

"Are they still for sale?" he asked.

"Don't you have a horse, John?" she asked.

"I have a good horse. However, he's got a sprain and I won't be able to ride him for a few days."

"Maybe I'll just give you one of the Arabians out there then. How would you like that, John?"

"What's the catch?"

"Come to work for me. I'll pay you well and give you either one of those horses, hand over a bill of sale. No strings."

"What exactly would I do for you?" Slocum asked.

"My father was killed down in Harrison, just the other side of the Missouri border. But I think he was set up by someone down there. Oh, I know Tolliver had a hand in it, but whoever killed my father had to know when he would be coming along that lonely, very hilly stretch of road to the north of Harrison. I want you to find out who betrayed me and set up my father."

"What makes you think you were betrayed, Miss Collins?"

"Whoever set my father up for his killing knew me and knew him. And I feel sure it was someone I trusted. Someone who was a friend, or that I thought was a friend."

"Any proof?"

Linda shook her head. "Nothing I can take to a magistrate. But before my father died, he said something to the driver who was with him."

"What did he say?" Slocum asked.

"He said, 'Friend.' Then he said, 'Black heart.' "

"Any idea what he meant by that?"

Linda shook her head. "It was very strange, but he must have thought it very important."

"Why?"

"Because my father said it with his dying breath."

6

Linda Collins sent her hired hand, Clyde, to the livery on Commercial Street to bring back Slocum's saddle and bridle in the wagon. Slocum stood in the paddock with Linda watching Clyde drive the wagon away.

"How was the funeral, Miss Collins?" Slocum asked.

"Quiet," she said. "Solemn."

"Many people there?"

"No, just Clyde and me, one or two friends. Why do you ask?"

Slocum hesitated. He wondered if he should tell Linda that he had met her sister that day. But now he was wondering if the lady who called herself Meg Collins really was Linda's sister. He thought he could detect a family resemblance, but he wasn't quite sure.

"Reason I asked," he said, "is that I met a woman at the hotel who said she was your sister. She said she was in town to attend your father's funeral."

"Meg? You met Meg?"

"She said that was her name."

"That bitch. She didn't come to the funeral. My daddy had no use for her. She's married to one of the Tollivers, and might even know all about how my father was killed. I mean, she may even have set him up."

"How could she do that? Was she close to him? I mean, your father?"

"When she wanted something from him, she was close."

"Well, I guess the lady was who she said she was," Slocum said.

"Did she know you were coming to see me?" Linda asked.

"Yes. She saw me reading that advertisement and came over to my table at breakfast this morning."

"Was she with a man named Ferguson?"

"They were sitting at separate tables. He came over too, and warned me about buying these horses from you."

Linda's eyes widened, and her face drained of color. She drew in a deep breath, held it for several seconds, then let it out again.

"Is something the matter?" Slocum asked.

"It's a wonder you're still alive," she said.

"Why?"

"Ferguson is a killer, one of Tolliver's hired guns. He and my sister have worked together before."

"How so?"

"I think she sets up men who get in Tolliver's

way, gets them to put their guard down so Ferguson can shoot them in the back."

Slocum decided not to tell Linda Collins about being ambushed by two people when he first came to her freight yard. It would only complicate matters that were already complicated enough.

"What does your sister's husband say about her being with a killer?" Slocum asked.

"Her husband is the one who told his brother about Ferguson and laid out the plan for her to work her charms on men so that Ferguson can gun them down."

"How do you know all this?"

Linda licked her dry lips. "She tried to get me to turn against my father and throw in with Tolliver. She even told me what she and Ferguson did for Tolliver."

"It's not a pretty situation," he said.

"No, it's ugly. Meg didn't try anything on you, did she?"

"What do you mean?" Slocum asked, his tone laden with innocence.

"Ask you to come to her house or offer to meet you at a saloon?"

"No," Slocum said, glad that he didn't have to lie, "she didn't do any of those things. She did invite me to the funeral, though."

"What?"

"She said she was going and would introduce me to you."

"That lying bitch."

"I guess so," Slocum said.

"She probably wanted to kill us both at the same time."

"Do you know why your sister turned so hard?" Slocum asked. "Of course, it's none of my business."

"That's right, Mr. John Slocum," Linda said, a sharp tone to her voice, "it's none of your business."

Slocum knew that that particular subject of their conversation was over. He walked up to the horse Collins was giving him and looked it over once again.

"I'll buy the other one from you when I finish up the job," he said.

"We can talk about that later," Linda said. "Right now, I want to give you instructions. Do you need a cash advance for expenses?"

"No. I can get by, Miss Collins."

"I'll give you a map to Harrison, Arkansas. It's a direct route, unlike the one Tolliver has. I want you to stop in Hollister, where we have a freight office. I'll give you a letter of introduction to my agent there."

"All right," Slocum said.

"Then, a day or so later, ride down to Harrison. We pick up our freight at Barnes and Son. Again, I'll give you a letter of introduction and all the particulars."

"And what exactly do you want me to do, Miss Collins? I know you told me once, but I want to be sure."

"I want you to find out who set up my father and who murdered him. Someone down there knows what happened. And I want to know who's loyal to me, and who's thinking of switching freight lines and going over to Tolliver."

"Don't you think it might be hard for a stranger to ask a lot of questions, especially about something this serious?"

"You may not have to ask any questions at all, John."

"Oh?"

"Once you tell these people you work for me, I'm sure they'll volunteer the information I'm after."

"Why didn't you send Clyde down there then? Or ask one of your drivers to question these people?"

"Good question," she said. "First of all, Clyde might be good at sneaking up behind you and laying you out cold because he's a very quiet man. He's not a thinker, though, and you look like a thinker to me."

"And what else? What about your freight haulers?"

"Those men are so rattled because of my father's death, they're afraid of their own shadows. Again, you don't look like a man who is afraid of very much."

"Good answers," he said.

"And those will have to do for now. I hear Clyde coming back with your saddle. Can you leave for Hollister today?"

"As soon as I get my bedroll and saddlebags from the hotel, I'll head south."

"Good. Come on back into the office and I'll get you that map."

Slocum was saddled up in less than a half hour, and twenty minutes later he was in the hotel lobby, standing at the desk.

"Is Miss Collins in?" he asked.

"She paid up and left this morning, shortly after you left, Mr. Slocum."

"Do you know where she went?"

"I presume she went back to her home in Rogersville," the clerk said.

"She comes here often, does she?"

"Quite often, in fact."

Slocum got his bedroll out of his room, along with his Greener shotgun and saddlebags. Before the sun set, he was heading south toward a town he'd never heard of: Hollister, Missouri. As near as he could figure, it was about forty miles away, perhaps less, and he knew he'd be sleeping under the stars that night. That was why he had stopped at a store and bought enough provisions to last him three days. Although he expected to sleep on the ground for only one night, the extra provisions were insurance in case he ran into something along the way he couldn't handle and might have to stay off the trail longer.

The road to Hollister was well defined, rutted here and there, thick with prairie grasses and wildflowers. He saw no other travelers coming his way, and he made sure to look over his shoulder in case he was being followed. The day was clear and sunny and he could see a long way. Well out of Springfield he could detect no rider in his wake, but he was not about to let his guard down.

The flat plain gave way to deep thick woods and the country became more hilly and rugged. The road wound through this terrain, and Slocum knew that he was now vulnerable, not only to an ambush, but to anyone following him. For he could no longer observe his backtrail, nor could he see very far ahead.

He was glad to have a good horse under him. Even though he had not stretched the gelding out, he knew it had good bottom and sound legs. He saw deer and turkey, and flushed doves in some of the few open places he passed through. He could take to such country, he thought. It reminded him of his home in Calhoun County, Georgia, with its deep woods and shadows, lots of wild game.

The country became even more rugged, and he saw towering bluffs where the road-builders had dynamited through the woods to cut a pass through limestone. He was traveling downhill, and marveled at the stark contrast between this part of the road and the part that streamed out of Springfield across the prairie. This was another world entirely, and he knew it could be a dangerous world for the unwary.

Late in the afternoon, the long shadows shrank and became dark puddles. He knew the sun had not gone down on the plain, but it would be dark in the woods long before the sun sank below the western horizon.

Slocum thought about riding on in the dark. But then he began to see woodcutter trails leading off the main road, and he knew how easy it would be to take one of those by mistake and become lost. He might lose more time than he would gain.

As it grew darker, he knew he would have to find a place to spend the night, a place where he could sleep and not worry about someone sneaking up on him in the darkness and shooting him in his bedroll.

He decided not to take one of the woodcutter trails. That would make him too easy to track. Instead, he looked for a place that offered both a hollow and a bluff, believing that would give him better choices for finding a safe place to spend the night.

As the daylight grew dimmer, Slocum spotted a promising place some distance from the road. He saw a high, tree-studded ridge atop a limestone bluff. He was certain that below it, he would find a deep wooded hollow that would afford him a hiding place that he could easily protect should someone try and sneak up on him during the night.

He turned off the rutted, washed-out roadway, and headed into the woods. He was careful to ride slowly and not leave a clear path behind him. He turned the horse every few feet, in a zigzag pattern, so that even a good tracker would have a difficult time following him.

It was rough going through thick timber, mostly hardwoods, oak and hickory, a few walnut trees, but there were cedar and gum trees too, and sumac grew wild with the dogwoods and redbuds that were no longer in bloom.

The darkness in the woods was deep and growing deeper as Slocum slowly made his way toward the limestone bluff, riding there by dead reckoning since, under the canopy of leaves, he could no longer see the ridge.

Finally, Slocum came to a hollow that ran parallel to the bluff. He hesitated, wondering whether to ride down into it and back out on the other side, or follow the ridge around it. If he was down in the hollow and someone was following him, he would be at a disadvantage. It was always best to keep to the high ground. He had learned that in the war, and he knew it was a solid axiom.

In that moment when he reined in the horse and was mulling over his decision, he heard the crackle of a branch underfoot. It could be a deer, he thought, or just the natural sound of a dead branch cracking at the change in temperature following the setting of the sun.

He waited, listening hard to see if that was all it was.

Then he heard another cracking sound, from the same direction. Either a deer was leaving its bed early, or someone was tracking him through the woods. He had cracked a few dead branches himself when he rode in, following that zigzag course.

Slocum rode to the highest point above the hollow. There was more light there, but he knew it wouldn't last long. He rode the horse behind some trees and peered down over his backtrail, hoping to see someone before it got too dark.

He saw nothing, and it grew very quiet. He was about to move to another spot when he realized he had nearly made a fatal mistake. A rifle shot cracked the silence, and he heard the snap of the bullet as it hit the bark near his head. Pieces of bark stung his cheek, and he ducked instinctively.

Then another rifle shot boomed from another direction and the bullet spanged off the tree, flinging bits of wood in all directions.

Whoever had followed him in there had him braced on two sides. If he didn't get out of there, the next shots would probably find their mark.

Slocum hauled the reins hard and turned the horse away from the trees. He headed straight down the hollow at breakneck speed. Two more shots rang out, and he heard the bullets whine and strike rock, ricocheting off like angry hornets.

In moments, he was in the darkness of the hollow, the horse thrashing through thick brush.

Slocum wondered if he could outrun his pursuers. For now, he knew he was safe, well below their lines of sight. But he knew they could trace his course by the noise the Arabian was making. The seconds ticked away, and to Slocum it seemed like an eternity.

And then he broke free of the depression that was the bottom of the hollow and he was on flat ground. The horse turned to avoid some trees, and Slocum glanced ahead.

There, in front of him, blocking his path, a massive bluff rose out of the foliage.

Slocum's retreat was blocked as if he had run into a wall at the end of a dead-end street.

7

Slocum was lost, and he knew it. The darkness had descended into the woods, and the deep hollows blanketed the bluffs and wiped out all landmarks.

He felt as if he had descended into a deep pit and there was no way he could get his bearings in that Stygian blackness that had enveloped him as soon as the sun set.

He rode along the edge of the bluff, bearing south by his reckoning. He walked the horse slowly and stopped often to listen. The two people who had shot at him were probably still on his trail. He had no doubt that they were heading in his direction, and that they were listening too.

A few faint stars appeared in the sky, but there was no moon yet. The country was rocky, hilly, and thick with trees. All of these conditions were obstacles to Slocum in the darkness, but they were also advantages. They kept him from being seen by the two shooters. As long as he kept moving, there was a chance that he would lose them in the deepness of night.

And he knew that at some point, he would have to stop and rest, perhaps sleep if he could. Otherwise, he was in for a long and sleepless night.

He thought he heard something crash in the woods above him. He listened, but there was no other sound. He continued riding, very slowly, and when he ran out of bluff, he angled to his left, hoping to keep parallel to the road he had left. In the morning, if his reckoning was right, he could find the road easily and be on his way to Hollister.

He wondered how he could have let two people catch up to him like that. He had seen no sign of them on the flat. Had someone been waiting for him? Impossible, he knew. No, he had been followed from Springfield. So, who had known he would be heading south to Arkansas? Linda Collins, of course, and her hired man, Clyde Bellows. Had someone been watching him when he left the hotel? Possibly. Probably, he reasoned. Maybe, he thought, the two shooters had already known somehow that he would be riding south and had gotten ahead of him.

But if so, he wondered, why hadn't they just ambushed him on the road? Were they that smart that they would wait until he left the road to kill him? Maybe. Perhaps they wanted to shoot him and leave his body where nobody was likely to find it for a long time.

He knew he was facing some pretty smart people. Smart people who were also very dangerous. Someone meant to kill him, and his first thought was that it was Pete Ferguson and Meg Collins Tolliver. He was pretty sure that they were the two who had tried to put his lamp out at the Collins freight yards. They were the only ones who knew he was going to look at those horses.

Slocum began to wonder what he had gotten himself into, and more than that, he was wondering whom he could trust. Every thought became magnified in the darkness. Every danger loomed greater in the silence of the night.

Slocum began to look for a place to bed down for the night. He knew he could not keep wandering through the woods, aimless, lost, confused, and hope to gain any ground or even elude his pursuers. He had already decided what he was going to do when he came upon a small creek. He looked up and saw that he was in a kind of draw, that there were high bluffs on either side.

He knew he had to find a place beyond the creek, for the noise of it would drown out any sounds of someone approaching his campsite.

He rode on, looking blindly in the dark for a place that would suit his purposes. He rode until he could no longer hear the gurgle of the creek, until he found a place where the silence was as deep as the woods.

He discovered a small open place, a little meadow, grassy, but empty of trees. Perfect, he thought. He dismounted and walked around it to determine its dimensions. Satisfied, he led the horse into the woods that fringed the small glade and tied the reins to a bush. Then he took his bedroll down from the saddle, stripping the horse of its saddle and blanket. He carried these things into the meadow, but not to the center. He carried them to the far side and laid them out in plain view. He laid the saddle at the head of the stretched-out bedroll and took off his hat, laying it to one side.

He made what he called a false camp. Anyone riding up in the darkness would see the outline and shape of the bedroll and saddle and think that he was sleeping there. When he was satisfied, Slocum walked back into the woods and led the horse some distance from the meadow, hobbling him at a place where there was plenty of grass to last him the night.

Then he took his Greener and saddlebags back to the edge of the meadow. He found a small copse of trees that he could lie down in without being easily seen. But he had a good view of the meadow and the false camp.

He set up the saddlebags and laid his Winchester and Greener across them, within easy reach. It was not the first time he had slept on the bare ground, but this was a better place than most. There was grass here, and once he had removed all the rocks, he found a comfortable place to stretch out and wait. He drew his pistol and set it to his side, within easy reach.

Anyone coming upon the false camp during the night would have quite a surprise if they opened fire on his empty bedroll.

Slocum lay down and listened. The horse was far enough away so that he could not hear him grazing, and Slocum was glad to know that he could not hear the creek either.

Slocum reached quietly into one of his saddlebags and dug out some hardtack and jerky. He munched quietly, listening to every sound. He washed the food down with water from his canteen until his belly was full. Then, after looking up at the stars for a few minutes, he closed his eyes. He listened intently until he fell asleep, but heard no sound.

Sometime before dawn, Slocum awoke. It took him several seconds to get his bearings. At first he didn't realize where he was, and then it all came back to him. He looked out at the meadow, lit now by moonlight. His false camp was still there and he could detect no sign that anyone had come there during the night. The moon was low in the sky, and he knew it would not be long before it began to get light.

He was stiff from sleeping on the ground, but he was dry. The dew had not yet begun to form on the grasses and his guns. He arose slowly, stiffly, and stretched to take out all the kinks in his bones and muscles.

He holstered his pistol and picked up his rifle. He walked quietly into the woods and saw that the Arabian was still there. It did not whicker when it saw him, but tossed its head in recognition.

"Good boy," Slocum said, and then walked back to his sleeping place next to the meadow. He found an oak tree and sat down, leaning back against it to wait for the sun to come up.

He had no idea where he was, but he was confident he could find his way back to the road. He had been in worse places.

Slocum ate again, just to keep something on his stomach. He wished he dared make coffee, but he knew such an act could prove fatal. He waited out the rest of the night, and when it was light enough to see, he got up from his seat by the oak tree and looked once more out onto the meadow.

Then he froze as he saw a branch move on the other side of the glade. He squinted to narrow his vision, isolate whatever had made those leaves dance. That was when he saw a rifle barrel snake up under the moving branch and level off. Behind the rifle, Slocum saw the shape of a man kneeling down, bracing himself against the trunk of a sturdy tree.

Slocum did not move, but watched in fascination as the man took a bead on the empty bedroll, took in a deep breath, and then pulled the trigger. The rifle barked and smoke belched from the muzzle. The bedroll twitched as the bullet ripped into it. The man got up and stepped out into the open.

Slocum raised his rifle and set the man in his sights.

"Hold it right there, mister," Slocum said. "And just let that rifle fall to the ground. You so much as swing it one way or the other and I'll drop you where you stand."

The man looked over at Slocum and slid the rifle down, butt-first, through his hands. When the butt struck the ground, he stooped slightly and laid the rifle down.

"Now walk away from it," Slocum ordered. "Toward me. Keep your hands up high where I can see them."

The man raised his arms and started walking toward Slocum. A pistol jutted from a holster on his belt, but he made no move to draw it. Slocum held his rifle steady and walked up to the man. He reached over and pulled the pistol from its holster, sticking it in his own belt.

"I don't know you," Slocum said.

The man said nothing.

Slocum looked him over. The man stood about five eight or nine, was dressed in loose, rugged clothing. He looked like a squirrel hunter, Slocum thought. He had a day's beard stubble shadowing his jaw and chin.

"Well, you're not Ferguson," Slocum said. "So you must be one of the Tolliver boys. Which one?"

Still, the man said nothing. He stood there, glaring at Slocum.

"Step back into those trees," Slocum said. "Ferguson might be close by, drawing down on me."

The man turned, and Slocum prodded him in the small of the back with the barrel of his Winchester.

"Are you going to kill me?" the man asked.

"Oh, you got a tongue," Slocum said. "I wondered if the cat had got it."

"Are you going to shoot me?" the man asked.

"I'm thinking very seriously about doing just that," Slocum said.

"That would be a big mistake," the man said.

"You thought I was in that bedroll. You were trying to kill me."

"I thought it was a varmint," the man lied.

"The only varmint I see around here is you," Slocum said.

"Play it your way," the man said.

Slocum told the man to stop once they were inside the trees, protected somewhat from anyone who might be watching from a long way off. "Turn around," Slocum said.

The man turned around. Slocum looked him over again, studying his eyes. The man didn't move his head, but his eyes were busy, moving around in their sockets, trying to look left and right.

"You think Ferguson heard that shot?" Slocum asked. "You think he's going to come up and save your sorry ass?"

"He ain't far," the man said.

"So you and Ferguson were hunting me down. I thought as much."

"You aren't as smart as you think you are, Slocum."

"I'm not the one facing the business end of a Winchester," Slocum said. "Now, get down on your knees."

"What are you going to do?"

"Kneel."

The man knelt down. Slocum put the barrel of the rifle snug against the man's temple. Then he pulled the hammer back. It made a loud click. The man's face drained of color. His hands began to shake.

"Look, Slocum, I'm only following orders. No harm done. Let me go and I'll light a shuck."

"Not until you tell me who you are and who sent you to kill me."

"I can't do that."

Slocum pushed on the rifle, putting pressure on the man's temple. The man began to sweat. Profusely. Beads of moisture seeped from under the lining of his hat and trickled down his face and into his eyes. He blinked at the stinging of the salt.

"You're just a hairsbreadth away from eternity," Slocum said. "All I have to do is give this trigger a little squeeze and your brains will be all over the bushes like ticks on a dog."

"Christ," the man swore. "You're a cold-blooded bastard."

"My guess is that you're Jasper Tolliver. I have no use for a man who'd send his wife to bed an enemy. Or a friend, for that matter."

"I ain't sayin' who I am."

But Slocum had seen the man's eyes flash at the mention of his name. He was now almost certain the man on his knees was Jasper Tolliver, Meg's husband.

"Well, maybe someone will find your body in here and identify you for your widow," Slocum said. "Frankly, I don't give a damn who in hell you are. You're just another backshooter as far as I'm concerned."

"Slocum, you don't know what you're getting into. Even if you kill me, you can't beat Karl. The stakes are too high. You've got a price on your head."

"Karl Tolliver? Your brother, you mean. Well, if

I have a price on my head, it's going to cost Karl Tolliver a little bit more than he expected to pay. Meaning your life."

Slocum pushed the rifle a little harder. The man at the other end of the barrel winced.

"So long, whoever you are," Slocum said, and started to pull the trigger, just enough so that the man could see his finger put pressure on it.

The man's eyes flared with a look of pure terror in that long, brutal instant.

8

The kneeling man's eyes filled with tears as he faced eternity. He could plainly see Slocum's finger squeezing the trigger.

"No, wait," he said suddenly. "You're right. I'm Jasper Tolliver. Please don't kill me."

Slocum let out a breath and eased his finger off the trigger.

"That's better," Slocum said. "You just bought yourself a little more time."

"What do you mean?" Tolliver asked. "Are you still going to kill me?"

"I might. It depends on what you have to say. For instance, where's Ferguson?"

"He's not here. We split up this morning."

"If you're lying, Jasper, I'll close your mouth permanently. You'd better be telling me the truth."

Slocum stuck the barrel of the rifle into Tolliver's neck, where the skin was softer.

"I am, honest. Ferguson rode on ahead to cut you

off if you got away and kept on going down to Hollister and Harrison."

"Get up, Tolliver," Slocum said. "You and I are going to take a little ride."

"Where to?"

"To Hollister."

Slocum walked Tolliver over to his saddle. He cut enough rope to tie Tolliver up so that he wouldn't run off or otherwise become a nuisance. Then he hefted his saddle and bedroll and marched his prisoner into the woods, where he set him against a tree while he saddled up the Arabian.

"Where's your horse, Tolliver?"

"About a quarter mile yonder in the woods."

"You'll walk there. I'll be right behind you."

"You're a bastard, Slocum, you know that?"

"I've heard that before. Now, move."

A little over a half hour later, Slocum was following the bound Tolliver as they rode through the woods. The road was about where Slocum figured it would be. Tolliver complained the whole way until Slocum told him to shut up. He held the reins to Tolliver's horse, but kept him close. If anyone was up ahead waiting for him, he wanted to be able to bring Tolliver up as a shield.

"Any idea where Ferguson might be waiting for me, Tolliver?"

"He could be anywhere."

"Well, if he shows, I'll drop you first, so you'd better holler if you see him before I do."

"I'm powerful thirsty," Tolliver said.

"You keep that in mind. You'll be a lot thirstier if I send you to hell."

"Damn you, Slocum."

And those were the last words Tolliver spoke until Slocum saw the land dip down and flatten out. He saw that the road now paralleled a large river.

"That the White?" Slocum asked.

"Yep. Hollister's just up ahead."

"You'd better pray that Ferguson doesn't show until we get where we're going."

"I don't know where he went. We ought to have seen him by now."

Slocum wondered about that. He figured Ferguson to be a mite smarter than Jasper Tolliver, and he also figured Ferguson was a man who liked to pick his own time and place to assassinate someone.

Soon, they rode into the outskirts of Hollister, which wasn't much, a bunch of clapboard buildings, a tavern, hotel, livery, mercantile, and other buildings he could not yet see.

"Slocum," Tolliver said just before they entered the town, "hold up, will you?"

"What for? So, Ferguson can draw a bead on me?"

"No. Something else. I don't think Ferguson is here. He wouldn't shoot you in town. That's not his way."

"What is his way?" Slocum asked.

"You don't remember me, do you?"

"No, I don't. Should I?"

Slocum's eyes narrowed as he looked at Tolliver. He tried to remember if he had ever seen the man before, but he saw nothing in his face to jar any recollections about the man.

"I rode with Quantrill, same as you."

"A lot of men did. I wouldn't brag about it if I were you."

"I'm not. I couldn't stomach some of the things Quantrill did."

"So what's the point?"

"The war was hell here on the border. It ruined families; it ruined me. I was a Union soldier, and I quit, joined up with Quantrill."

"Why?"

"I thought Missouri should have joined up with the South. I hated the Union. I deserted. The outfit I was with had a battle not far from here."

Slocum thought back to that bloody time. General Sterling Price had promoted him to captain and assigned him to Quantrill, whose burning and pillaging of Lawrence, Kansas, forced President Jeff Davis and General Robert E. Lee to sever all relations with him. But Slocum had learned a lot while riding with Quantrill, and had nearly lost his life while under his command.

"I remember when you came to Quantrill," Tolliver said. "You had a reputation as a sharpshooter at Gettysburg, and we knew General Price put a lot of store in you."

"That's all past now," Slocum said.

"You got even better with the Colt pistol," Tolliver said, "and that word got around too."

"What's your point, Tolliver?"

"The point is that Ferguson rode with Quantrill

too. He's the one who got me to desert the Union Army. So he knows your reputation."

"And?"

"And I think he's a mite scared of you. I mean scared of meeting you face-to-face with either rifle or pistol."

"Ferguson's a damned backshooter anyway, isn't he?"

"I guess so. But he brought me along on this one, and he usually works by himself. I figure he'll be behind some rocks somewhere between Hollister and Harrison, just waiting for you to ride by so he can put you in his sights."

"Why in hell are you telling me all this, Tolliver?"

"I'm hoping you'll show me some mercy. I don't want to die. And if you take me all the way to Harrison with you, and Ferguson kills you, he'll surely kill me too."

"Well, you can put your mind at ease, Tolliver. I'm not taking you with me to Harrison. I'll give you back your bullets and you can ride back to Springfield."

"Really?"

"Yes. You're just extra baggage to me after I stop off in Hollister. But if I ever see you on my trail again, I'll shoot you dead. Is that clear?"

"Right clear," Tolliver said.

"Are you ready to ride back to your little woman then?"

"You won't ever see me again, Slocum. I promise."

Slocum considered letting Tolliver go right then

and there. If he was right about Ferguson, then he
had no further use for Tolliver. But he'd have to
watch out when he rode to Harrison. For Ferguson
would surely be waiting for him, as Tolliver had
said, behind some rocks. And wasn't that where
Linda Collins's father had been murdered? Somewhere around the border between Missouri and Arkansas, she had said.

"What kind of rifle does Ferguson use?" Slocum
asked.

"It's a Spencer repeater."

"I reckon he's good with it," Slocum said.

"He's got a Creedmore scope on it. You won't
have a chance once he gets you in his sights, Slocum."

"What kind of man are you, Tolliver? To ride
with a man like Ferguson, who would just as soon
kill you as me?"

"Ferguson don't like loose ends. He learned that
in Kansas, from Quantrill. Don't leave any witnesses."

"But he works for your brother."

"Karl is scared of him too, if the truth be known."

"You're a fine bunch, all of you. I'm going to cut
you loose now, Tolliver. You head back home and
keep in mind what I told you. I mean it. If I see you
again, I'll kill you."

"I have no doubt about that."

Slocum untied Tolliver and put the ropes back in
his saddlebags. He handed Tolliver the bullets he
had taken from his rifle and pistol. "Don't you put

these back in their chambers until you're an hour back up that road to Springfield."

"I won't," Tolliver said, taking the bullets and putting them in his pocket. "And thanks."

"Go on and get," Slocum said.

Tolliver rode back the way they had come. Slocum watched until the man was out of sight, disappearing into the trees and between the high bluffs above the White River. Satisfied, Slocum turned the Arabian and rode into Hollister, keeping to the shady side of the street.

Slocum rode to the Red Fox Saloon in the center of town. It was a combination tavern, stage stop, and shipping point for Collins Freight, and was the place Linda had told him to go and introduce himself to the owner.

There was a hitch rail and after he dismounted, Slocum wrapped the reins of his bridle around the rail. He patted the Arabian. "We'll get you some grain pretty soon," he said.

Slocum looked up and down the street. People were walking along, and some folks were crossing the road. There was another street that entered the main one at an angle, and most of the activity seemed to be on that street. It was such a small town that, if you blinked your eyes when you rode through, you'd miss it.

He stepped inside the tavern and stood to one side of the door, waiting until his eyes adjusted to the light.

Slocum saw a pool table to his left, where four men were playing. There was a door beyond the

table. To the right was a long bar against the wall,
and along the opposite wall were tables. The narrow
room widened at the back into a larger room. Men
and women sat at some of the tables drinking beer
and whiskey. Slocum saw no familiar faces at any
of the tables or among the pool shooters.

There were two bartenders working, a man and a
woman. The woman was beautiful, with long golden
curls framing her face, bright blue eyes, and a smile
that could melt a man's heart.

"Well, don't just stand there, stranger, come on
in and make yourself at home," the woman said with
a smile that was both radiant and genuine.

"Don't mind if I do," Slocum said, striding to the
end of the bar nearest him, but against the wall.
From there, he could see the front door, the door at
the pool room, and most of the patrons in the narrow
part of the room. He sat down. The beautiful woman
came over.

"What'll it be?" she asked.

"You have any Kentucky bourbon?" Slocum
asked.

The woman smiled.

"A man after my own heart," she said. "Old Taylor suit you?"

"That will be fine."

"Six bits," she said.

Slocum let out a low whistle.

"Too steep for you, mister?" she asked. "I've also
got Taos Lightning, some local rotgut, and the house
whiskey, made from grain full of rat droppings and
Lord knows what."

"The Old Taylor will be fine," Slocum said, plunking some coins on the counter.

He watched as the slender woman with an hourglass figure and ample breasts walked down the bar and reached down, pulling out a bottle of Old Taylor. She didn't have to dust it off, but it was almost full. She brought it to the end of the bar, along with a shot glass. She poured the shot glass to the brim.

"Not much call for this," she said, "but it's what I drink. When I do drink."

"And when do you drink?" Slocum asked.

"When there's good company to drink with."

"I'll buy you a drink then," Slocum said. "If you're Justine Hanson, that is."

The woman smiled.

"I don't think we've met, have we?"

"No. I'm John Slocum. Linda Collins sent me down from Springfield. Told me to look you up."

"Pleased to meet you, John Slocum, and I will have that drink. Four bits."

"Four bits?"

"I get a discount," she said, then laughed. Her laugh was as bright as her eyes, and just as genuine as her smile.

Justine poured herself a drink of whiskey, not so generous as the one she had poured for Slocum. He laid some bills on the bar. She moved one away from the others, but didn't take it to the cash register, which sat on the back bar.

"So, you must be the man Linda was looking for," she said. "A man not afraid to buck the Tollivers."

"You know about that?"

"I know her father was killed and she sent a message down a few days ago with one of her drivers. Said she was going to hire a brave man to bring her father's murderer to justice. I take it you're that man."

"Maybe. I'm just looking around right now."

"And you're going to Harrison?"

"Yes. Maybe tomorrow. First, though, I was wondering if you saw Pete Ferguson last night or this morning."

"You'd better take a slug of that whiskey, John, before I tell you about Pete Ferguson."

Slocum looked at her closely. Justine Hanson was dead serious.

He took the drink, and felt the raw whiskey burn his throat, take hold in his belly, and send a warmth through him that was like a shot of morning sun.

"Well, at least your eyes don't water," she said. "I think I'd better have a swallow before I tell you about Pete Ferguson."

"It must be bad," Slocum said.

"It sure as hell ain't good," Justine said.

Then she drank her whiskey, draining the shot glass in one gulp.

9

There were no tears in Justine's eyes either, but the light in them took on a kind of smokiness that Slocum noticed.

"Maybe I ought to buy you another one," Slocum said.

"No, that'll do me, thanks. Lean a little closer, John. I don't want what I'm going to tell you to go any further than your ears."

Slocum leaned over the bar and Justine did the same, so that they faced each other eye to eye.

"Ferguson was here?" he asked.

"He came through early this morning. I didn't see him, but Charlie, the other barkeep, told me about it. He was looking to hire someone to put your lamp out. I should have recognized you when you walked in, because Ferguson gave a good description to Charlie, offered him fifty dollars if he would shoot you dead when you walked in here."

"And did Charlie take Ferguson up on his offer?"

"No," she said, "but somebody did."

75

"Who?"

Justine shook her head. "I don't know. I wish I did. But Ferguson later told Charlie he'd found someone else. If I were you, I'd be damned careful while you're in town. Somebody's got a bullet in his gun with your name on it."

"But you don't have any idea who's gunning for me," Slocum said.

"No, I truly don't, John."

"Can you give me a line on who might have killed Linda's father? How it happened?"

"I think we ought to go in the back where we can talk," she said. "Too many big ears here. I'll bring the bottle if you want to have another drink or two."

Slocum smiled. "My throat's still a mite dusty," he said.

He followed Justine after she came from behind the bar. She walked to the table furthest in the back. She waved Slocum to the seat with its back to the wall, so he could see anyone coming into that section. There was no one back there, and it was dark and cool with thick rock walls, a small lantern burning over the fireplace for light.

Justine set the bottle on the table. Slocum finished the drink he had and poured himself another. Justine had brought her glass with her too, but when Slocum offered to pour her a drink, she shook her head.

"What can you tell me about Jasper Tolliver?" Slocum asked.

"Spineless," she said. "He's Pete Ferguson's shadow, though. Meg wears the pants in that family.

She doesn't even go by his last name, still calls herself Meg Collins."

"I think Ferguson and Tolliver tried to kill me last night," he said. "I jumped Tolliver this morning, sent him back to Springfield."

"You should have killed him. He'll do anything that bitch wife of his tells him to do."

"I gather Tolliver and Ferguson fought together in the war."

"Yes. They both deserted their Union outfit, and joined up with Quantrill up in Kansas. Their outfit was wiped out in a battle not far from here, over in Forsyth. They're both scoundrels. Were you in the war, John?"

"I was." He didn't tell her he rode with Quantrill. He thought that might cloud the issue. "Tolliver thinks Ferguson might be waiting to ambush me between here and Harrison."

"He might. But he bought himself a little insurance when he came through here this morning. He hired somebody to gun you down, I know that. But I don't know who."

"But you know something about Linda's father, how he got killed, and where."

"That's a funny thing, John. Nobody was supposed to know that Linda's father was riding up from Harrison that day. Linda knew, but I didn't. Nor did Chad Barnes, or any of the other drivers."

"I'm supposed to meet Chad Barnes in Harrison," Slocum said.

"Yes, he runs the freight company there, Barnes

and Son. Linda's father didn't tell him he was riding up that day either."

"But somebody knew," Slocum said.

"Somebody was waiting for him just south of town, near the Arkansas border. About eight miles from where we sit. The driver picked his body up when he was making his regular freight run from Harrison to Springfield."

"Maybe Ferguson, or somebody, just camped along the road, out of sight, until Collins came along."

"No, I don't think so. Whoever killed Linda's father knew he was coming that day. In advance."

"Why do you say that?" Slocum asked.

"Because her father told everyone he was going to return by way of Forsyth, take the ferry over. Anyone who wanted to kill him would have had to wait miles from where her father was killed."

Slocum said nothing. He was beginning to get a clear picture of what had happened that day and how secretive the Collins family had been. So Linda's father must have known he was a target, and had done all he could to avoid losing his life to a bushwhacker.

"You may find out more when you see Chad Barnes down in Harrison," Justine said. "He and his son were in a position to know if there were any suspicious characters hanging around the freight yards."

"I mean to talk to him and his son."

"He has a couple of daughters too, John. They may know something."

"Linda didn't mention them."

"She wouldn't. You're a very attractive man, John, and the Barnes girls are both single, both very beautiful. And both are quite seductive."

"Why would that make any difference to Linda? She and I hardly know each other."

Justine laughed. She pushed her glass toward the bottle and nodded. Slocum poured her a drink until she held her hand up to stop him.

"Linda too is a beautiful young woman. Unmarried, eligible. She's still looking for the right man. Competition is fierce in these Ozark hills. There just aren't that many good men around. Most of the unmarried men are lawless scoundrels."

"How about you, Justine? Are you married?"

"I was. My husband was one of those killed over in the Battle of Forsyth. His bones are in the White River, with a lot of other good men."

"I'm sorry."

"I stopped crying about Jake a long time ago, but thanks."

"Maybe I'd best go and put my horse up, see if I can find a bunk for the night. I saw a hotel across the street."

"We serve food here, if you're hungry. It's cold, meat and vegetables, but it's filling. Are you hungry?"

"Starved," he said. "Will you join me?"

"I'll sit with you, unless we get busy, which is not likely. The next freight wagons won't be coming through until tomorrow, from Harrison. But there should be one coming down from Springfield tonight, late."

"I'll be back for that meal. I want to get my horse out of the sun and get some grain in him."

"I'll be here," she said.

Slocum put the horse up in the livery stable, gave orders to grain him, and got a room in the White River Hotel, a second-floor room that looked down on an angled street from one window and on the main street from another. The clerk had not paid any special attention to him, and Slocum had seen nobody suspicious in the lobby.

When he walked back to the Red Fox Tavern, he studied the people he saw, and none paid him any undue attention. By then, he was hungrier than he had been, and he looked forward not only to a good meal, but to seeing Justine again.

Just before Slocum was about to step into the tavern, something caught his eye off to the left, where the freight yard was located. There was a small building there, a loading dock, a corral, and some farm implements alongside the structure. Behind the building, there was a line of trees, and he knew there must be a creek running through the town.

He had seen someone on the creek bank duck behind some trees. He stopped and waited, his right hand hovering just above the butt of his pistol.

He waited for the man to reappear. Perhaps, he thought, someone was fishing from the bank, and had just moved to another spot. He thought he had seen a man, but it could have been a boy.

Slocum walked away from the Red Fox and made

a beeline for the freight office. He kept his right hand close to the butt of his pistol. When he had put the building between him and the man hiding in the trees, he edged along the side of the building, heading toward the creek.

When he got to the back of the building he could see the trees clearly. He hugged the building for cover and called out.

"You there. Behind the trees. Step out so I can get a good look at you."

There was no answer. And no movement.

"I know you're there," Slocum said. "Step out, or I'm coming in after you."

Behind him, Slocum heard the *snick* of a hammer cocking back. Too late, he realized he'd been tricked. The man must have heard him coming and circled around the opposite side of the building.

Slocum knew he had less than a second before he took a bullet in the back that would finish him for good.

In that instant, his mind raced at a furious speed. He could almost see, in his mind, the man squeezing the trigger. And in that instant, Slocum could see down the long tunnel of eternity.

And there was nothing but blackness at the end of it.

10

Slocum squatted and whirled, drawing his pistol just as he heard the explosion from a big-caliber gun. He saw a man standing ten yards away, his upper body shrouded in white smoke.

Slocum cocked his pistol and squeezed off a shot as he backed in behind the building. He heard the smack as his bullet struck home. The man cried out and, a second later, Slocum heard a thud as a heavy body struck the ground.

Slocum peered around the corner of the building and saw the man sprawled on his back. He got to his feet and rounded the corner, cocking his pistol just in case the man meant to shoot at him again.

But the man's pistol lay on the ground several inches from his hand. Slocum looked down at him and swore in disgust. The man had a hole in his gut, just above his belt buckle, and blood was pumping out of it in crimson gushes like a fountain.

The man gasped for breath and looked up at Slocum with glazed, pain-filled eyes.

"Tolliver, you sonofabitch, why in hell didn't you ride on back to Springfield like I told you?"

Tolliver's mouth moved, and finally a rasping sound came out.

"Ha—had to try one more time." Tolliver's eyes batted open and closed several times.

"That was your mistake." Slocum kicked Tolliver's pistol away. "You're done for."

"I—I know. I—I can feel it. It's real bad, ain't it?"

"Can you move your legs?" Slocum asked.

As he said that, people began pouring out of the Red Fox Tavern and streamed toward him.

Tolliver shook his head.

"You probably don't feel much pain either, do you?"

"No," Tolliver said.

"Bullet probably clipped your backbone, you dumb bastard."

Justine rushed up to Slocum and stared down at the wounded man.

"He came back," she said softly.

"He tried to backshoot me."

"Well, you got him, John. You got him real good."

"I hope I won't have a tangle with the law here over this," he said.

"No. We have a town marshal, but he's a drunk, and is probably asleep. He starts early on the bottle."

"Well, it was self-defense."

"I'll take care of it," she said. "He's dying, isn't he?"

Tolliver made a gurgling sound in his throat. His eyes flared wide for a moment and then clouded over, turned agate with the frost of death.

"Not anymore," Slocum said.

"Charlie, get some help and carry Jasper to the undertaker's. I'll mind the tavern."

"Yes'm," Charlie said. The others came closer to gawk at the dead man as Justine led Slocum back toward the Red Fox.

"This will be good for business this afternoon and tonight," she said. "All of those people there will spread the word and the bar will fill up."

"A hell of a way to make a dollar," Slocum said.

Justine saw to it that Slocum was served a full meal of cold beef, boiled potatoes, bread, beets, and string beans. While he ate, the two of them talked.

"There will be hell to pay over Jasper Tolliver's death," Justine said. "Karl and Ivan, his brothers, will want your blood."

"It seems to me they don't need to have a reason for that. They're out to kill me anyway."

"But now you've taken away their brother, and the Tollivers are clannish, to say the least."

"Jasper was a fool," Slocum said. "I spared his life and he didn't have sense enough to accept the favor."

"I think he was ashamed to go back and tell Meg that you bested him. She was awful hard on poor Jasper. And by the way, Meg will want your hide tacked to the barn too."

"You think he was afraid of his wife?"

"Jasper was afraid of his own shadow. But yes,

Meg is an ambitious woman, and she's terribly jealous of Linda. Linda was always closer to her father's heart than Meg was, and Linda was also her mother's favorite."

"Nothing so fierce as a woman scorned, eh?"

Justine laughed. "You know your women, John."

"Not nearly well enough," he said.

Slocum finished scraping his plate and pushed it aside. He patted his belly in satisfaction.

"Get enough?" Justine asked.

"More than enough."

"I hope the meal doesn't affect your senses, John."

"What do you mean?"

"You may have killed Jasper Tolliver, but there's still a man in town who's gunning for you."

"I haven't forgotten. I wish I knew who it was. Do you have any idea? Am I looking for a big man, a little man, a farmer, a shopkeeper?"

Justine sighed. "I can't help you there. I wish I could. People here in Hollister are cash poor. Since the war, nobody seems to have two nickels to rub together. A man like Ferguson can offer a man fifty dollars and draw a crowd."

"But he didn't do that. He picked out someone. Didn't he?"

Justine shrugged. "I don't know. He found someone willing to take the chance."

"Maybe, when word gets around about Tolliver, whoever wanted that bounty will have second thoughts."

"Don't count on it, John." Justine fixed Slocum

with a look that told him she was taking the hired gun seriously and that she was concerned about him.

He thought of Justine as he walked back to the hotel. He fed another cartridge into the cylinder on his Colt as he crossed the street. He looked up at every building, at every window, and at every passerby. He did not want any more surprises such as the one Jasper Tolliver had given him.

Once at the hotel, and back in his room, Slocum lay on the bed to rest, to think. He was forming a picture in his mind of what he was facing. When word got back to the remaining Tolliver brothers that he had killed Jasper, they were liable to come after him in force. He couldn't let that happen.

Meanwhile, he still had an obligation to Linda to find out who had killed her father and bring the murderer to justice. It appeared that the freight route from Springfield through Hollister to Harrison was lucrative enough to bring out the greed in Karl Tolliver. At lunch, Justine had told him that the Tolliver route went through more rugged country and took longer.

Apparently, according to Justine, Tolliver had never made Collins an offer for his freight line. Instead, he had used threats and intimidation to close him down. She said she had been threatened herself, and she knew Chad Barnes had been warned about doing business with Collins Freight. But Tolliver wanted too much money to do business with *his* outfit, and the other freight handlers didn't want any part of him.

It was an age-old conflict, Slocum knew. One man

wanted what another had, and was willing to commit murder to get it.

He had learned a great deal from talking to Justine. Much of the freight hauled up to Springfield was produce, crops produced by Arkansas farmers. But Collins also handled goods made by individuals and companies, and these traveled both ways. There was a lively trade in the Ozarks between the two states, and Collins Freight had a firm grip on it. They promised speed and reliability and, according to Justine, they delivered. Tolliver was forced to take a lesser cut of the pie since his route was longer and did not cover major farming areas.

So there was a lot at stake, and apparently Karl Tolliver was greedy enough to want it all for himself. And he was willing to go to any lengths to get what he wanted.

Slocum napped, dozing with one eye open, listening to the sounds of Hollister during the lazy afternoon. The noises picked up toward evening and when he looked out the window, he saw wagons streaming toward the freight loading dock, all of them laden with fresh vegetables bound for Springfield. The vegetables were all crated up. He saw other wagons bearing freshly made barrels of various sizes, and others that were laden with newly made furniture—tables, chairs, chests of drawers, and even beds. One wagon was full of crates labeled "dulcimer" and "guitar." So the people in the hills also made musical instruments, Slocum thought, as well as furniture. The town, which had seemed like a small backwater place, was now teeming with activity.

Slocum dug out his straight razor and soap, shaved, brushed his frock coat, put a sheen on his boots with an oilcloth, and made ready to leave his room and head for the Red Fox Tavern.

Before he left his room, Slocum walked to the window once again and looked down on Hollister's main street. This time he was looking for anything or anyone out of the ordinary, for something that was out of place or someone who didn't seem to fit in with the rest of the townfolk or the farmers and manufacturers bringing items to town that would be freighted to Springfield when the evening freight haulers came through.

Most of the people he saw were either with the wagons, or were walking to some predetermined destinations. They all seemed to have someplace to go, or something to do. But in the shade of a shop with an overhanging roof, Slocum saw a man who didn't seem to belong to the throng. He was smoking a cigarette and, from the looks of it, he had been standing there for some time, since there were butts scattered around his boots. The man had a pistol stuck in his waistband. As near as Slocum could tell it was a converted Remington New Model Army that had once been a percussion six-gun and had been modified to shoot cartridges.

The man was unshaven and wore a battered hat. He looked to be in his late twenties or early thirties. His hand kept going to the butt of his pistol, as if he was reassuring himself that it was still there, tucked in under his belt.

Slocum stood to one side of the window where he could see without being seen. He was waiting for the man to do something that would give him away, would give Slocum some idea of why he was standing there.

He did not have to wait long.

The man put out his cigarette and reached into his shirt pocket for the makings. As soon as he pulled out the sack of tobacco, the man looked up toward the hotel. His gaze went directly to Slocum's window. The man brought out some papers and extracted one, then began to roll a cigarette. Then he stuck the quirly in his mouth and looked up at Slocum's window once again.

That was the sign Slocum had been waiting for. As the man struck a match, his gaze drifted over to the hotel entrance. He lit the cigarette and continued to gaze at the entrance and touch the butt of his pistol.

"All right," Slocum whispered to himself. "You're waiting for someone to come out of the hotel. And it's probably me. Let's see if we can't end your waiting."

Slocum left his room and walked down the stairs to the front desk. He looked out the window, and saw that he could not see the man standing across the street. Which meant the man could not see him either.

"Is there a back way out of the hotel?" Slocum asked the clerk, an older man he had not seen before.

"Sure. There's another entrance on the back street there too."

"Thanks," Slocum said, and walked around the desk to another part of the lobby. He saw the other entrance. Before he went outside, he looked out a small window to see if anyone was waiting on the other side of the street. There was no one there. He opened the door and stepped out onto the street.

He looked both ways and saw only people walking past the shops and stores, some going in, some coming out.

Slocum walked quickly up to the end of the block, away from the hotel, rounded the corner, and went to the main street. There, a cart was crossing, and he walked on the other side of it and followed it across, shielding himself from the waiting man.

Then he went behind the buildings, saw an alleyway, and walked down it nearly to the end of the block. He hadn't noticed the name of the store when he had looked out his hotel window, but he knew it was the third store from that end of the street. He stopped there, and saw that there was a back door.

He went up the steps and tried the door. It was locked.

There was a space between the buildings, though, and Slocum walked back down the steps, thinking to go between the buildings and come up on the man, brace him, and disarm him.

He was halfway to the main street when a man stepped into the open space. It was the same man he had seen watching the hotel. This time, he had his pistol drawn and aimed straight at Slocum.

Slocum started to turn and go back the same way, hugging the building. As he turned, he saw another man step into view from the alley. This man too had a pistol aimed at Slocum.

"It's all over," the man on the street side said, and Slocum heard the metallic click of the hammer cocking back, locking into place.

"Die, Slocum," said the other man, cocking his pistol.

In that instant, Slocum knew he was a dead man.

11

Slocum had only an instant to decide what to do. He was braced by two killers, and they had him in a narrow box from which there was no escape.

If he shot one, the other was bound to shoot him in the back. Which man was the better shot? Which was the faster? Slocum didn't know, and there was no time to think about it.

Slocum threw himself facedown on the ground facing the gunman on the street. He drew his pistol and cocked it, just as the man fired his own pistol. The bullet sizzled over Slocum's head. Slocum fired, and saw the gunman crumple. Then he heard a cry, and turned to see the gunman in the alley stiffen and throw up his arms. His pistol went flying as his knees buckled and he fell to the ground, a bullet high on his chest, near the throat.

"Big mistake," Slocum said aloud, knowing neither man could hear him.

The gunman who had fired had not reckoned on Slocum being on the ground. His bullet had passed overhead and struck the second shooter in the chest.

Slocum got to his feet and walked toward the street. He looked down at the man who had been hired by Ferguson to kill him.

"What's your name?" Slocum asked. He could smell whiskey fumes on the man's breath.

"Roy Betz. I'm the town marshal."

"You've got lead in your brisket," Slocum said. "You might live if a sawbones can dig it out."

"Damn you."

"Who's the other man? You shot him, you know."

"My deputy, Frank Duggan. Is he dead?"

"You got him square in the chest. I doubt he's breathing."

"Fifty damn bucks," Betz said.

"Which you won't collect. Do you know where Ferguson is?"

"He—he headed toward Harrison this morning."

A crowd began to gather. People looked at Slocum as if he were an assassin in their midst. He ejected the empty shell from its chamber and pushed a fresh cartridge in to replace it.

"This man tried to kill me," Slocum told the crowd.

"Why, he's the town marshal," a woman said.

"And a piss-poor one at that," Slocum said.

The woman's mouth opened and she put a hand over it, obviously horrified by his crude language.

"Betz here shot his deputy. He missed me, and hit Duggan back there."

"Well, at least neither of 'em was married," one man said.

Slocum took one more look at Betz. His shirt was bloody around the hole just below his chest. Blood bubbled up out of his mouth. Slocum stepped over Betz and looked at the people who had gathered around. "Better get this man a doc if you want him to pull through," he said. "I doubt much can be done for him, though."

"Who are you, mister?" a man asked.

"Someone who wants to stay alive," Slocum said, and passed through the crowd, which parted to let him through. He heard the buzz of conversation rise up behind him as he made his way across the street to the Red Fox Tavern. He was calm outside, but his belly was quivering from the close call. He needed a shot of bourbon to clear his head. He had been lucky this time, but he wondered if his luck would hold when he ran into Ferguson.

The tavern was full of noise and people. It was obvious to Slocum that no one inside had heard the two shots. As Justine had predicted, they were talking about the shooting that morning. Now, he thought, they'd have more to talk about once word got out about the marshal and his deputy. Justine would do some business this night for sure.

She was busy, Slocum saw. She was down at the far end of the bar, pouring drinks. As Slocum walked toward her, the talk died down and every head turned in his direction.

"That's him," someone whispered.

"Damn. He's a big 'un."

"He's dangerous," said another.

Slocum stood behind the last man seated and looked over at Justine.

"Whiskey?" she asked.

"When you get a minute," he said. "I'm in no hurry."

"Bill, get up and give John Slocum your seat," Justine said. "You've sat there long enough."

The man she had spoken to turned and looked at Slocum. His eyes were wet and rheumy from drink. He gave Slocum a lopsided smile and oozed his buttocks off the barstool.

"Sure, have yoreself a seat, John Slocum. And I'll, by God, buy you a drink."

"That won't be necessary," Slocum said.

"Be my everlastin' pleasure," Bill said.

Slocum sat down. "I should buy you a drink for giving up your seat."

"It's my everlastin' pleasure."

Slocum smiled. Justine set a glass in front of him and poured him a drink. She smiled as he put money on the bar top.

"That's taken care of," she said. "Bill's buying you a drink."

"I think I'm going to head out tonight, Justine. Something's come up."

"So soon? I thought you were going to stay the night. I was hoping we could have supper together at the hotel."

"I'd better light a shuck," he said, swallowing the glass of whiskey. It went down as smooth as water.

"What happened?" she asked.

"I think I've worn out my welcome here in Hollister. I just shot your town marshal."

"What? Roy Betz?"

"I believe that was the man's name. His deputy, Frank Duggan, is dead too, although I didn't kill him."

Justine's face registered the shock she felt. Her jaw dropped and her mouth opened in an O of surprise. She drew in a deep breath to help herself recover.

"I would never have figured Roy'd have the guts," she said.

"He was working on whiskey courage from the smell of him."

"That weasel."

"They were pretty smart, old Roy and Frank. They had me in a tight spot. It could have gone either way."

"Well, they won't be missed much, John."

"It looked to me like there might be a lynch mob forming out there."

Justine laughed. "Nobody's ever been lynched in Hollister. But you're right. The mob has a mind of its own. I'm worried about you riding down to Harrison at night, though. Ferguson might be waiting to drygulch you."

"Can he see in the dark?"

Justine laughed again. "No, but he can hear. And I wouldn't doubt but that someone from town has already ridden south to tell him about Roy Betz."

"Ferguson must have a lot of friends in Hollister."

"More like a lot of people afraid of him. I

wouldn't put it past one of our good citizens to try and curry favor with that killer."

"I'll keep my eyes and ears open."

"You've got a good forty or forty-five miles, maybe more, to Harrison. And the road passes through some pretty rugged territory. There are lots of hills and curves in the road."

"Any quicker way, or easier way to get down there?" Slocum asked.

Justine shook her head. "That's why this route is so valuable. You don't have to cross any rivers by going this way. You'll pass Bear Creek Springs and Bear Creek, but that's manageable. Collins built a bridge over the creek."

"All right. I'll be on my way. Thanks for the hospitality, and the information."

Justine reached across the bar and put her hand on top of Slocum's. "Be careful," she said. "And hurry back. I still want to have supper with you. Someday."

"Someday," he said. He finished his drink and walked through the crowded saloon. There was still plenty of daylight left, and he felt like riding into some new country.

Slocum paid up at the hotel under the suspicious eyes of the desk clerk, walked to the livery, and saddled the Arabian. He made sure his Greener was loaded and within easy reach inside his bedroll behind the cantle.

He took the road south. A sign read: HARRISON, ARKANSAS, 50 MILES OR MORE. Slocum laughed. Well south of town, he saw the Collins freight wagons rumbling toward him. He pulled the horse off the road and waited for them to pass. The drivers waved at him, but they lashed their horses, and he knew they had no intention of stopping to talk to a stranger. There were four large wagons all bearing the legend COLLINS DRAYAGE, SPRINGFIELD, MISSOURI. None of them were full, but they were all hauling freight and each had a man with a shotgun sitting next to the driver.

He figured they had more wagons in Hollister if they needed to add any to the train. They probably wouldn't change horses in Hollister, though.

It was almost dark when he saw the wagons, and a few moments later, he was riding through hills deep in shadow, and before he knew it, the darkness was on him. He had passed the Arkansas border and the land was flat for a time, then began to descend and rise where the road cut through. The horse was well rested and showed no signs of fatigue.

Slocum stopped often to listen and rest the horse. The road was easy to see under starlight, and there were no clouds to dim what light there was. He knew he was making good time. He ate along the way, chewing on hardtack and jerky, washing the food down with water from his canteen.

Then the road dipped deep into a low spot and wound around through the middle of a valley. Then it began to climb steeply, and he knew that this was the most dangerous place so far.

He looked for cover, but there was very little. Just a few trees every so often just to the side of the road. He was in the open, exposed, and even the

Arabian appeared to be getting nervous.

Slocum was still some distance from the top, climbing the steepest part of the road, when he heard the rifle shot. It cracked the stillness like a bullwhip snapping, and he heard the high whine of a bullet as it passed close. The bullet struck the ground a foot behind the horse's hind legs.

He had seen no flash, and knew the shooter must be concealed in a thick clump of trees somewhere above him.

Reacting quickly, Slocum turned the horse off the road and in the next few seconds, he and the animal were plunging down a steep draw that bled off the road. The horse picked up speed and Slocum held on for dear life.

Down, down, down, the horse raced, out of control, picking up speed down the steep draw. Slocum expected to hear one of its legs snap as it struck a rock or got a hoof stuck in a hole.

Two more rifle shots barked, and he saw the muzzle flash the second time. He knew where the rifleman was now, but it did him little good. He couldn't stop the horse if he wanted to, and he knew that once he did stop, he'd be easy pickings for the shooter.

The horse reached a bottom where a small ridge blocked its way. Slocum hauled back on the reins, then turned the horse back into a stand of brush and dismounted, jerking the Winchester out of its scabbard. He crabbed back to the hump in the bottom and found a rock jutting out that he could use both for cover and to steady his rifle.

He jacked a shell in the chamber and took aim at the spot where he had seen the muzzle flash. He squeezed off a shot, then moved, hunching down and skirting the small ridge to another spot that shielded him from the rifleman above him.

Seconds later, the shooter fired again, and the bullet spanged off the rock where Slocum had been and ricocheted off at an angle, whining like some leaden banshee into the night.

Slocum saw the flash from the shot, and quickly levered another cartridge into the chamber and fired off a shot, allowing for his night vision, aiming a little high to be sure. Then he ejected the brass hull, slid another bullet into the chamber, and crawled along the bank away from where he had left his horse. Another rifle shot boomed from the bald above him and hit the ground behind where he had been with a dull thunk.

Slocum did not fire again, even though he had seen the orange flash from the muzzle. It was a good two hundred yards and he was shooting uphill, which challenged his marksmanship. He waited, listening for sounds of any movement.

He hugged the bank so he would present no silhouette to the bushwhacker. He waited and listened.

All he could hear was the sound of his heart pounding.

12

Slocum's beating heart blotted out all other sounds for a long time. He waited for the next rifle shot, but none came. In the darkness, he groped around for a rock and found one, near where his knee was pushing into the bank.

He pulled the rock from the earth and crouched down even lower. When he was satisfied that he could not be seen, he threw the rock over the mound and down deeper into the gully. It hit some brush and made a crashing sound.

Again, he waited for the ambusher to shoot at the sound. But the next thing he heard was a thrashing high above him, and then the sound of a single horse's hooves as they struck the road. He heard the horseshoes plunk on stones. Gradually, the sound of the hoofbeats diminished and faded away into silence.

Slocum carefully walked back to where he had left his horse. He did not mount up, but led the horse through the brush at the bottom of the draw. He began to walk up toward the bald, a place where a farmer had cleared the land of trees and brush, taking an angle that would lessen the steepness of his climb. He didn't want to go back to the road just yet and risk riding into another ambush.

When he reached the edge of the bald knob, Slocum skirted it until he was safely among the trees that bordered it. There, he mounted up and, keeping the bald in sight, rode parallel to the road. Again, he stopped often to listen, but heard no telltale hoofbeats or noises from the road.

He knew he was in for a long night and a long ride as he rode through the hardwoods to the other side of the bald knob that crested the steep hill. He stopped there and surveyed his options. If he continued on the same path, he would descend into another hollow and have another rugged climb ahead of him. The horse would tire before the sun came up if he rode up and down the many hills, and he might not reach Harrison before daylight.

In the distance, Slocum saw a lone farmhouse at the edge of another cleared field. He knew he could not go that way. A farm meant dogs and dogs would bark and betray his presence. He knew he would have to angle over to the road again, have to chance it, or he would wander these endless hills and lose his way in the darkness.

He reloaded his rifle and put it back in its scabbard, hoping he would not have to take it out again real soon. He clucked to the horse and turned it toward the road. He traveled up another small hill and down the other side, then up another one before he found the road. At least it ran flat for as far as he could see, although it made a bend a couple of hundred yards from where he came back on it. That was where he would have to be on his guard, he knew.

He traveled slowly, stopping often to listen, and when he came around the bend in the road, he hugged the trees off to the side. He didn't figure Ferguson was any better at shooting in the dark than *he* was, and it was pitch black now that clouds had moved in and covered the moon and most of the stars. That, he thought, was a blessing.

On he rode, through the night, and toward morning, he crossed what he took to be Bear Creek, which was down at the bottom of a long hill. Then the road climbed again and circled some rugged low bluffs. But the climb was not steep, and the horse had watered at the creek and found new legs. The clouds had thickened and there was a smell of rain in the air. He passed places where he saw distant farmhouses, dark square shapes in the vastness of night, no lamps burning at that early hour.

He rode on, fighting off sleep and weariness, fighting to keep his senses alert in case Ferguson jumped him again.

At the top of the hill, close to the time when the sun would rise, Slocum saw that the land lay flat for as far as he could see in the predawn murkiness. The road stretched straight and long, but he knew it was no less dangerous just because it was straight. Ferguson could still be waiting somewhere up ahead, his rifle at the ready.

There was a creek running alongside the road, but

some distance from it. If Linda's directions had been correct, he should find the Barnes outfit right on the main road into town. According to her, the office and buildings were just this side of Harrison before he got to the town proper. That, he knew, would be another dangerous place. Ferguson just might be waiting for him to show up, ready to blow him out of the saddle before he reached his destination.

It was almost noon when Slocum began to see signs of the town, little stores and dwellings off to the side of the road. Dogs barked at him, cats slinked from porches and crept underneath the buildings, wide-eyed women in long dresses stared at him, and men looked at him blankly as if he were a crazy man escaped from some institution for the insane.

Just past noon, Slocum saw the sign BARNES & SON atop a building off to the side of the road. It was a large freight yard with lots of wagons stacked next to the creek, corrals, stables, a couple of buildings that he took to be warehouses, and farmers and workmen waiting to unload their goods to be shipped over the border.

And no sign of Ferguson, Slocum thought with relief.

A man appeared on the office porch. He was wearing a pistol, loose summer clothing, and flat-heeled boots. Slocum swung down out of the saddle and hitched the horse to the rail, looping the reins over the cedar pole.

"Howdy," the man on the porch said.

"Howdy."

" 'Pears you come a long ways. I figger from Hollister, or Springfield."

"Both," Slocum said. "Are you Chad Barnes?"

"I am. And who might you be?"

"The name's John Slocum. Linda Collins sent me down."

"Ah, I thought you might be the man. Didn't know who it'd be, but Linda said she was going to bring her pa's killer to justice. She told me to expect someone to pay me a visit. Come on inside and set. Hungry?"

"I could eat, Mr. Barnes."

"Call me Chad. There's a cafe just down the road. Me and you can go there and talk."

"I'd like to hear what you think about the Collins murder, Chad. Any suspicions? Anybody you think might have done it?"

Barnes led Slocum into a private office behind a long counter. A woman sat at a desk working through papers. She looked up briefly, and Slocum's eyes met hers for a brief moment. She was pretty, but since she was sitting down, he could see nothing more than her face and bosom. She was slender, though, with dark hair and brown eyes.

"That's one of my daughters," Barnes said as he closed the door behind Slocum. "You'll meet her later. I have another daughter who's not here and a son who's outside in the yard taking in freight to be hauled to Springfield today or tomorrow."

"Do you keep a regular schedule?" Slocum asked as Barnes waved him to a chair.

"We try not to, because of the trouble we've had with the Tollivers."

Barnes sat down behind a large cherry-wood desk covered with papers, a couple of spindles with more papers skewered to them, pencils, a quill pen and well, an oil lamp, and a paperweight made of what looked like a chunk of lead or iron.

There were maps on the wall behind the desk, and the other walls were filled with bric-a-brac, samplers and Currier & Ives prints. A large Waterbury clock dominated one section of wall near the door.

"Then how do you account for someone waiting at the Arkansas border for Collins?"

"I can't account for that, unless the killer just camped out there and waited for Collins to come by."

"But you don't believe that," Slocum said.

Barnes shook his head. "No, I'm afraid not. Whoever killed Ralph Collins knew that he was coming that day, and knew exactly when."

"So someone down here got the word out to the killer."

"I don't know who it could be."

Slocum studied the man. Barnes seemed sincere, and maybe he didn't know who had sold Collins out. But he might not have looked too closely at his own people either. Someone in Tolliver's outfit wanted Collins out of the way and had taken great pains to eliminate him.

"Where's this food place?" Slocum asked.

"Mama's Kitchen. Just down the road. I'll tell my

son Lenny we're going there. Do you have a place to stay while you're in town?"

Slocum shook his head.

"Then I can put you up. I have a large house. It won't be any trouble."

"That's kind of you, Chad."

"My pleasure."

Barnes told his son, Lenny, that he and Slocum would be at Mama's Kitchen. Lenny and Slocum shook hands after they were introduced. Lenny was a slender young man, perhaps nineteen or twenty, not yet filled out to adult proportions. He was taller than his father and twice as skinny.

Barnes and Slocum walked to Mama's Kitchen, a small cafe two blocks from the freight yards. Beyond, Slocum saw a large sign on a building surrounded by other buildings and corrals, wagons, and such.

"That Tolliver's place?" Slocum asked.

"Yep." Barnes looked disgusted. "The competition."

"He seems to be doing business."

"Not enough to suit him."

Mama's Kitchen was nothing more than a large room with tables and a small counter. The kitchen was in back, and Slocum's mouth watered at the smell of food cooking. There was no Mama there, he learned. Mama was a swarthy Italian named Pepino Guido, a very fat, amiable man who, with his daughter, Gina, did all the cooking and waited on tables. The place was full and no one paid Barnes and Slocum much attention. Pepino shooed two men away who had finished eating and seated Barnes and Slocum at a wall table.

"Steak and taters for me, Pepino," Barnes said. "Slocum?"

"The same."

"I fill 'em up," Pepino said, laughing.

"Does Tolliver's bunch eat here?" Slocum asked Barnes.

"Yes, but they don't bother us. They're good boys. It's Karl and his brother, Ivan, who are the troublemakers."

"Do they come down much?"

"Ivan does. Haven't seen him this week, though. He generally comes down every couple of weeks."

"Do you know a man named Pete Ferguson?" Slocum asked.

"Just about everybody round here knows of Ferguson. Few claim to know him. I've had him pointed out to me a time or two, but I'd be hard put to spot him if he walked up to my office porch."

"Linda seems to think Ferguson killed her father."

"I've heard much the same. Ferguson is a hired gun for Tolliver. At least that's what I've heard. He doesn't show his face much. I've never seen him up real close."

"So if he was here in Harrison now, you wouldn't know about it," Slocum said.

"There's so much talk and gossip about that man, I wouldn't know what the truth was. My men say they've seen him around the freight yards, but I never have. Nor has Lenny. He's like a shadow. Sometimes he's there, sometimes he's not."

"Well, I've seen him up close. Met him, in fact."

"You don't say."

"In fact, he gave me a warning. And I think he and another Tolliver, Jasper, have been trying to kill me to keep me from coming down here to see you."

"Jasper is a no-account, just like his brothers, but he's not much of a man, I hear. Odd thing is that he's married to Linda's sister, Meg, and that Meg is a piece of work. Not at all like her sister."

"Meg's a widow woman now," Slocum said.

"Oh? Did Jasper die?"

"He died of blood poisoning up in Hollister," Slocum said.

Barnes looked across the table. Recognition flickered in his eyes. "You? You killed Jasper Tolliver?"

"I had no choice in the matter, Chad. He just wouldn't give up on me."

"I'll be damned. Slocum, you're quite a man to buck the Tollivers. They'll put a big price on your head now."

"I think they already have."

"Well, they'll up it some if you killed Jasper."

"Have the Tollivers tried to buy you off?" Slocum asked with a suddenness that caught Barnes by surprise.

"Sometime ago they tried to get me to switch my business from Collins to them. I turned 'em down. Since then, they've more or less threatened me."

"What does 'more or less' mean?"

"I mean Ivan Tolliver flat told me that if I didn't throw in with them, I'd be a dead man."

"They didn't scare you," Slocum said.

"Oh, they scared me, all right. But they made me mad too. Linda's father was a decent, honest man. I figured I owed him my loyalty. He didn't deserve to be shot down like a dog."

Just then, Slocum saw a man come into Mama's Kitchen, a man he'd never expected to see there. The man had a pistol in his hand and, as Slocum stared at him, he brought the gun up, aiming it straight at him.

Barnes turned and saw the man at the same time.

"Hey," Barnes said, "ain't that . . ."

Someone yelled, "Look out!" and most of the diners dove for the floor. The pistol roared, filling the room with smoke and flame.

Barnes never got to finish his sentence. But Slocum knew the name that was on his lips, the name of the man who had come in and fired his pistol, shooting to kill.

It was Pete Ferguson, and no other.

13

Ferguson fired his pistol at Slocum, but just before he squeezed the trigger, Chad Barnes rose up and stepped in front of Slocum as if trying to protect him. He caught the bullet and went down hard, hitting the floor like a sack of meal.

Slocum drew his pistol, but before he cleared leather, the front door closed and Ferguson was gone. The room erupted in a hubbub as men got to their feet and rushed to the door, clogging it up so that Slocum couldn't get out to see where Ferguson had gone.

"Guido," Slocum said as he knelt down to look at Barnes, "if you know a sawbones, send someone to fetch him quick."

"I send for the doctor," Guido said, his face the color of paste.

"Damn," Barnes muttered as Slocum bent over him. "That was right dumb of me."

"It sure as hell was," Slocum said. "Let me take a look."

He turned Barnes over and breathed a faint sigh of relief. The bullet had missed the vital organs. Barnes was in a bad way, losing blood, but his position when he got hit had probably saved his life. The bullet had ripped along one arm and slammed into his right hip, just about where his leg joined his torso. The bullet was lodged in the fleshy part of the hip and would have to come out. But it would take a skilled surgeon to remove the bullet without killing Barnes.

"You lie real still, Chad," Slocum said. "Guido's sent someone for a doctor."

"Did he get away?" Barnes asked.

"Clean," Slocum said.

Finally, the restaurant was almost empty as the other patrons had managed to get through the door. Guido and his son stood there with a couple of other men.

Slocum looked up at Guido. "Did you know the man who shot Chad Barnes?"

"I know who he is," Guido said. "He is Pete Ferguson."

"Did anybody go after him?"

Guido shrugged and raised both arms, his hands turned palms up. "I don't think so," he said.

The doctor arrived within fifteen minutes, and some men came with an Army stretcher and waited outside.

"Hmm," the doctor said. His name was Harvey Leeds, Slocum found out, and he had been a battle surgeon in the war. "Bullet's lodged in his buttock.

Won't take much to get it out. But you'll be laid up for a time, Chad. Sorry."

"That's okay, Doc. Lurlene can run things."

"I expect she can."

As if summoned by mention of her name, a tall, slender woman came striding into the cafe. She wore expensive boots and black pants that fit her figure tightly. Her blouse was flame red and she wore a red ribbon in her hair. She had a riding crop in her hand, and the blunt spurs on her boots attested to the fact that she had been riding when she got news of her father.

"What's going on here?" Lurlene demanded as she walked into the room. "Harvey, is that my father there on the floor?"

The doctor seemed to shrink before her scathing glance.

"He took a bullet," Leeds said. "I'm going to have to move him to my office and take it out."

"Who the hell's responsible for this?"

Slocum stood up, faced the woman. She glared at him, her dark eyes seeming to flash with lavalike fires.

"You," she said. "Did you shoot him?"

"Lurlene," Barnes said, his voice weak. "This is John Slocum. I offered to take him in for a few days. He works for Linda."

"I want an explanation," Lurlene said. "Mr. Slocum, what do you know about this?"

"I think your pa took a bullet meant for me," Slocum said.

"Well, that's a damned shame," she said. "What

did you do? Duck behind him when the shooting started?"

"Lurlene, no," Barnes said, his voice just barely above a raspy whisper.

"You be quiet, Chad," Dr. Leeds said. "Guido, have those men bring that stretcher in. I don't want Chad to lose any more blood and that lead has got to come out."

Lurlene supervised the removal of her father, barking orders, demanding carefulness. When the wagon pulled away, with her father and the doctor in it, she turned back to Slocum, her eyes still flashing.

"You," she said, "if you've finished filling your sorry gut, come with me back to the office. I want to get to the bottom of this."

Guido shrugged when he looked at Slocum and turned away.

"What do I owe you for the lunch, Mr. Guido?" Slocum asked.

"Mr. Barnes, he pay for it. You go."

Lurlene stalked out of the cafe. Slocum followed her since he had nothing better to do. And besides, Lurlene Barnes fascinated him. He watched as she deftly mounted a tall black horse that looked every inch a thoroughbred. It had an English saddle, but she didn't ride like a woman. She straddled it like a man, and whopped the animal lightly on the rump with her crop.

"I'll see you in my father's office," she said as she rode away at a gallop.

"Mister," one of the men outside said, "that's

some woman yonder. She chews men up and spits them out like they was so much dirt."

"That's the kind I like," Slocum said, and started walking toward the Barnes & Son offices.

It was too bad Ferguson had gotten away, he thought, and he felt badly about Barnes taking a bullet that might have been meant for him. But he didn't feel guilty about it. Maybe Ferguson was a poorer shot than people gave him credit for. He had damned sure missed his intended target.

Slocum thought it was odd that Lurlene showed so little concern for her father's condition. She had been more interested in finding out who had shot him. He thought she would have gone with her father to the doctor's place, to see after him, to hold his hand and sympathize with his injury. But no, she was all business, as cold as a banker looking at red ink in an account ledger.

The office was empty, except for Lurlene. She sat behind her father's desk like a black widow spider in the center of its web.

"Come in, Mr. Slocum, and take a chair."

Slocum sat down facing Lurlene and crossed his legs. He could sense that she was sizing him up from the way her gaze raked him from head to toe.

"You look like a drifter," she said. "And that horse out there, is it yours?"

"It is."

"I recognize it as one of Linda's. Did you buy it from her?"

"I did."

"So you say. Have you got a bill of sale?"

"I do."

"Let me see it," she said.

Slocum dug through his pocket and found the bill of sale. He'd thought it might come in handy. He leaned over and put the paper on the desk in front of Lurlene. She picked it up, scrutinizing it with a thoroughness born of suspicion. She handed the paper back to Slocum.

"And you say you work for Linda Collins."

"She hired me."

"To do what? Get my father shot?"

"Miss Barnes, I don't see any need for sarcasm here. I didn't get your father shot. Nor did he get himself shot. A man named Pete Ferguson barged into Mama's Kitchen and fired a shot, presumably at me. Your father got in the way."

"You think Pete was trying to shoot you?"

"It's a possibility. Maybe he wanted to shoot both of us."

"Pete doesn't usually show his face at a shooting from what I hear."

"I've heard that too. He's more of a bush-whacker."

"What makes you think that?"

"He and Jasper Tolliver sure as hell followed me down from Springfield trying to kill me."

"I didn't hear anyone mention Jasper being at Mama's Kitchen."

"No, Jasper will be pushing up daisies right soon."

"He's dead?"

"As a doornail, Miss Barnes."

"You kill him?"

"Deliberately," Slocum said.

"So, you're not only a drifter, you're a hired gun."

"I'm neither, Miss Barnes. Linda asked me to look into her father's death. It seemed like the thing to do, and the pay's good. I was down in Missouri to buy horses, but mine went lame, so I had some time on my hands while my horse heals up."

"Well, have you found out anything about the death of Ralph Collins?"

"You mean about his murder," Slocum said.

"He could have been killed by a stray bullet from a hunter. These hills are full of hunters, Mr. Slocum."

"I think we all know who murdered Collins," Slocum said. "I'm wondering who set him up."

"Set him up?"

"Whoever murdered Collins knew where he was going and when he was leaving."

"Harrison, you mean."

"Yes. Somebody down here tipped off Ferguson and he was waiting to drygulch Collins."

"Seems to me you'll have to prove that, Mr. Slocum. And before you make any accusations."

"I just got here today, Miss Barnes. I've got a ways to go before I figure it all out. But I will figure it out."

"You sound very sure of yourself, Mr. Slocum."

"Murder will out, as they say."

"Oh, a Shakespeare lover."

"He did have a way of turning a phrase."

"Yes, well, I'm going to honor my father's promise."

"What's that?"

"To put you up at our house. If you're ready, I'll take you out there. You can board your horse in our stable while you're figuring out what you have to figure out."

"That's very kind of you, Miss Barnes."

"You might as well call me Lurlene. And may I call you John?"

"I'd be both honored and pleased," Slocum said.

"Follow me then, John."

Slocum couldn't be sure, but he thought she put a sarcastic twist on his name when she said it. Maybe that was just her way, a form of protection against men who might want to see what she had under her skirt.

Lurlene got up from her chair, and was rounding the desk when Slocum stopped her with a question that had been bothering him ever since he'd first seen the woman.

"Don't you want to look in on your father first, Lurlene?"

She stopped and glared at Slocum. "Doc Leeds is the best physician and surgeon in Arkansas, John. I trust him to give my father the best treatment. Meanwhile, the business he started must go on."

"Whether your father lives or dies," Slocum said.

"Whether my father lives or dies."

With that, she swept through the room and out the next so fast Slocum had to trot to catch up with her. He watched her mount her spirited black horse, and admired the way she took command of the animal with just her presence. He climbed aboard the Arabian gelding, and caught up to her before they left the freight office's lot.

"We live across the creek," she said. "Up on that ridge yonder. It's handy to the freight office and yet gives us peace of mind because we can't see the squalor of Harrison."

"You don't like Harrison?"

"Harrison is a town full of bad memories of the war, just like all the rest of the towns along the Missouri border. The Yankees pillaged and plundered us and some of us have still not recovered from the shock of it."

"You sound bitter, Lurlene."

"Were you in the war? Of course you were. You're about the right age. Just don't tell me you fought on the Union side. No, you aren't a damn Yankee. With that slight accent, you're either from Alabama or Georgia. I'd guess Georgia. Well, you know none of that war was fair to the South, and some of us down here still feel the boot of the Yankee conqueror on our necks."

"Do you always answer your own questions, Lurlene? And yes, I'm from Calhoun County, Georgia, and I fought against the North, but I don't carry grudges."

"You don't? You should. I do, and everybody down here does. Harrison is a fine little town, but we're in the shipping business because the money's in the North, in Missouri. It sure as hell isn't down here."

"And you want to be where the money is, right?"

Lurlene laughed harshly. "Money may not be everything, John, but it's way ahead of whatever's in second place."

"The love of money is the root of all evil, Lurlene."

"So, besides being a gunman, you're a philosopher, eh, John?"

"I don't think of myself as a gunman. Or a philosopher either. Someone else said those words long before I did."

They rode over the creek and to the top of the long ridge. The road led to a large gate that was open. Beyond, on a small hill, a large house commanded a view of the valley below. To Slocum it looked like one of those mansions he remembered from boyhood, tall and stately, with Doric columns and a large porch. It might have been a house transported from Georgia before the war, one of those he'd seen when he, his father, and his brother had hauled cotton from the large plantations to the cotton gin.

"You don't like me much, do you, John?"

"I haven't decided yet," he said.

"Good. I like a man with an open mind."

He wondered if that was true. To him, Lurlene appeared to be a woman used to having men grovel at her feet. He doubted if she really valued any of his opinions.

He decided, though, that she was a woman who bore watching closely. Very closely.

14

Lurlene and Slocum were met at the door by Lurlene's sister, who was just leaving. "I just came home for a quick bite of lunch, Lurlene."

"Well, you'd better get back down there. I didn't tell Lenny I was leaving the office."

"Oh, Daddy can manage without me."

"Charity, have you met Mr. Slocum?"

"Well, I saw him talking to Daddy before they went down to Mama's Kitchen."

"John, this is my baby sister, Charity."

"Pleased to meet you, Charity." Slocum noticed that Charity had dark brown eyes like Lurlene and her brother, but her hair was sandy-colored, not brown like her siblings. She seemed reserved and mousy, unlike her sister.

"Pleased to meet you, Mr. Slocum. Did you have a nice lunch with Daddy?"

"Daddy's at Doc Leeds'," Lurlene said. "He got shot."

Charity's face fell. She was obviously stricken

with the news. For a minute, Slocum thought she was going to cry.

"Oh, no! Is he all right? What happened?"

"You'd better go find out for yourself when you finish work. I don't believe anything's going out today."

"No, not until tomorrow. But we should see some wagons come in from Springfield this evening, and I'm expecting three wagons up from Crowley sometime this afternoon."

"Run along, Charity. Mr. Slocum will be staying with us for a day or two."

"I'll go see Daddy," Charity said, and disappeared from the porch. A few minutes later, Slocum saw her driving a buggy down the road toward the office while Lurlene was showing him the living room.

"If you'll come upstairs, I'll show you your room. Then I'll show you where to put your horse up while you're here. I think you can find everything you need. If not, there's a woman who cooks and keeps house for us. She lives out back with her husband. He does all the outside work here. Their names are Betsy and Don Pritchett. I won't be back until early this evening."

"Where will you be?" Slocum asked.

"That's none of your business, John. Just make yourself at home and I'll tell Lenny you might be talking to him."

"How do you know that?"

"Well, you're investigating, aren't you? I expect you'll want to talk to my brother. He keeps all the hauling schedules."

"Yes, you're right. I will want to talk to him. Probably this afternoon."

"Well, there's not much of that left." They walked down a hall and Lurlene opened a door. "This is your room," she said. "Mine is right next door, so I hope you don't snore."

"I wouldn't know," Slocum said.

"Well, I'll bet your wife knows."

"I'm not married."

"No? Well, I'm not surprised."

Slocum said nothing. He didn't want to feed Lurlene's penchant for sarcasm any more than he had to. She showed him the house where the Pritchetts lived and the stables, which were nicely kept.

"Good-bye, John," she said as he was leading his horse inside. "I've much to do."

"I suppose I can find Dr. Leeds' place all right? I want to look in on your father today, see how he's doing."

"Oh, yes, anyone can tell you where to find Doc Leeds. Bye."

Slocum watched her walk away, and let out a sigh. If there was ever a self-assured woman, he thought, Lurlene Barnes was certainly a perfect example of one. She left a big emptiness in her wake, and the faint scent of an expensive perfume.

Slocum unsaddled the Arabian, fed and curried him, then walked around to get a feel of the Barnes place. His impression was that they lived well, probably better than most of the people in Harrison. They obviously shipped goods not only to Springfield, but probably to Little Rock and other places too. If so, they were thriving, and that probably made the Tolliver family very envious.

He walked back to the house, and saw more evidence of wealth in the downstairs rooms. These were well furnished and appointed. He wondered what had happened to Chad's wife. He had heard no mention of her, and there were no pictures of her where he would have expected them to be. There were pictures of Chad, Leonard, and the girls, and the grandparents on Chad's side. Not a trace of a Mrs. Barnes or her family anywhere.

It was late afternoon before Slocum got the Arabian saddled up again and rode into town. He did not go to the freight office, but rode to Mama's Kitchen instead.

Inside, he asked Guido a pointed question. "Did anyone who saw Barnes get shot see which way Ferguson rode when he lit a shuck?"

"One man say he see Ferguson ride to Tolliver's. And then he rode into town."

"Do you know where Ferguson lives or stays when he's in town?"

"He drinks at a tavern downtown. It is called The Razorback. It is on Spring Street. I think he stays in a room out back."

"Thanks, Guido."

Slocum rode past Tolliver Freight, but did not stop there. They did not look very busy, though, and he saw no familiar faces among the men smoking out by one of the loading docks.

Slocum found The Razorback easily. It was a block off the town square. He saw that there were some small houses in back of the tavern, but he saw no horses at any of them. He rode back out front and hitched his horse to a ring, set in the ground in front of the establishment. He walked inside and stood for a moment to adjust his eyes to the darkened room.

There were only three or four men inside, and one blowsy woman seated at the end of the bar talking to the bartender. Slocum found a table that afforded him a view of the front and back doors. Ferguson, he noticed, was not there, nor had Slocum expected him to be.

The bartender walked over after a few minutes. He seemed in no hurry to serve Slocum. The woman at the bar turned and eyed the newcomer, and then lit a cigarette and turned away.

"We got beer and whiskey," the bartender said.

"Do you have Kentucky whiskey?"

"I might."

"Genuine Kentucky?"

"We don't get much call for that."

"Well, I'm calling for it."

"I'll see can I find you a bottle. Six bits. On the table."

Slocum laid a dollar on the table. The woman turned and looked at Slocum again. He had seen her kind before, cadging drinks any way they could. After the bartender brought the bottle and a glass, took Slocum's money, and gave him back a quarter, the woman got off the bar stool and walked over.

"Mind if I sit down?" she asked.

"Go ahead," Slocum said.

"My name's Kitty. What's yours?"

"Slocum."

"Slocum. That's a funny name."

"You can call me John."

"I will if you buy me a drink of that prime whiskey. I'm a little down on my luck, John."

A stern glance from the bartender prompted Slocum to place another dollar on the table. Then he poured Kitty a drink after she emptied her glass.

"What brings you to Harrison, John?"

"I'm looking for someone. Maybe you know him."

"I might. What's his name?"

Slocum kept his voice low so the other patrons and the bartender would not hear him. "Pete Ferguson."

"Pete? Sure, I know him. He lives out back in the middle house."

"Have you seen him today?"

"He was just here 'bout an hour ago. Bought me a drink and said he had to go do something."

"Did he say where he was going?"

"No, he never talks about what he does. But he said something funny."

"What was that?" Slocum asked.

"He said he had to make a trade."

"A trade?"

"Yes, that's what he said."

"And you don't know where he was going to make this trade?"

"He said something about—let's see, what was it? Something like doing an act of charity."

Slocum pulled a cheroot from his pocket, struck a match, and lit it. He couldn't figure Ferguson doing any acts of charity or kindness for anyone. He had already shot a man, and was hunting for Slocum. Was he thinking about going to where Barnes was laid up and finishing the job? Putting Barnes out of his misery? An act of charity in his mind perhaps.

"Do you know where Doc Leeds lives or has his office?" Slocum asked Kitty.

"Why, sure, he's a few blocks off the square on Maple Street. You can't miss it. He's got a sign out front."

"I'll buy you another drink, Kitty, then I have to go."

"Won't you have one with me?"

"No, maybe later."

Slocum paid the bartender, got directions from Kitty to Doc Leeds's house, and left the saloon. He rode around the square, up two blocks to Maple, and turned left. He dreaded what he might find, but the house was quiet and he hoped his hunch about Ferguson was wrong.

He tied his horse to a tree and walked up on the porch. The door was open and when he walked in, he saw that the living room was a waiting room for the doctor's patients. There was a man sitting there holding his jaw, and a woman with a small baby in her arms. They both looked up at Slocum.

"Is the doc in?" he asked.

"He's in the back with a patient," the woman said.

"With Chad Barnes?"

"Why, yes, he sure is."

Slocum went through the door and down the hall. There were several rooms. At the far end was a small hospital. Doc Leeds and a female nurse were working on Chad Barnes, who lay on his stomach.

The room smelled of raw alcohol, liniment, and blood. Both the doctor and his nurse wore surgical masks over their mouths.

"How's he doing?" Slocum asked Leeds.

"Good. We stopped the bleeding and I'm getting the last chunk of lead out of Chad's butt. The bullet splintered on his arm, which probably saved his life." Leeds didn't even look up. "I'm putting in the last of his stitches. In a week or two, he'll be good as new."

Chad seemed to be in a stupor, but he blinked his eyes and looked up at Slocum. "Nice of you to stop by," he said in a slurred tone of voice. "I'm goin' to be okay."

"Doc," Slocum said, "has Pete Ferguson come by?"

"No, why?"

"I don't know. I've been tracking him and he said something about . . ."

Before Slocum could finish his sentence, the door burst open and Lurlene rushed into the room.

"Slocum, you bastard," she said. "What in hell are you doing here?"

"I was looking in on your father."

Lurlene was waving a piece of paper.

"Do you know what you've done?" she asked.

"Nothing that I know of. Why?"

"Charity's missing, and I know that Pete Ferguson has her. I'll bet my bottom dollar on it. He knocked Lenny out with the butt of his pistol and kidnapped my sister."

"What?" Barnes said. Still lying on his stomach, he turned his head to face his daughter.

"That's right. And he left a note, Daddy."

"What's the note say?" Barnes asked.

Lurlene glared at Slocum. The look on her face was venomous.

"I'll tell you what it says. It says that he'll exchange Charity for John Slocum. He's giving us twenty-four hours to bring Slocum to Tolliver's or he says we'll never see Charity again."

"Damn," Barnes said. "That makes it right tough."

"Not for me, it doesn't," said Lurlene. "I wouldn't take a hundred Slocums for my sister. Slocum, you'd better give yourself up, or I'll deliver you dead to Pete Ferguson."

The room filled up with silence as all eyes fixed on Slocum.

15

Dr. Leeds finished stitching the wound in Chad Barnes's buttock and the nurse bathed the stitches in alcohol. "You'll have to continue this outside the operating room," Leeds said. "My patient needs rest and not aggravation."

"Go on, Lurlene," Barnes said. "Do what you can to get Charity back. I'll be all right."

"Daddy, get well quick," Lurlene said, and turned on her heel to leave the room. The doctor took Slocum by the arm and escorted him from the operating room.

"Watch out for Lurlene," Leeds whispered. "She's a wildcat."

Slocum nodded, but said nothing. Lurlene was waiting for him on the front porch of the doctor's house. It was obvious that she was fuming. She waved the piece of paper in her hand at Slocum and started right in on him.

"You're to blame for this, you know," she said. "If you hadn't stuck your nose into our business, my sister would still be at her desk working, and not in the clutches of that—that man Ferguson."

"Hold on, Lurlene," Slocum said. "First of all, your troubles started long before I got here. And second, I had nothing to do with your sister's kidnapping. And if you think I'm going to walk into Tolliver's and give myself up in exchange for Charity, you're a lot dumber than I take you for."

"Oh, you unreasonable bastard," Lurlene spat out. "I hate to think of what Ferguson might do to Charity while you stand by and twiddle your damned thumbs."

"Can we go someplace else to talk? I doubt if Doc Leeds appreciates us arguing on his porch."

"You meet me back at the office, Slocum. And right away."

"Why can't we ride over there together?" he asked.

"Because I'm going to stop by Tolliver's and give those bastards a piece of my mind."

"Whoa there, Lurlene. That won't do any good and it might get you into trouble. You're not going to solve a damned thing by flying off the handle like this."

"It's not your sister, so what the hell do you care what happens to her?"

"I care. And I feel somewhat responsible, but not in the way you mean. I should have seen it coming."

"What do you mean, you should have seen it coming?"

"I was trying to get a track on Ferguson, and I heard that he told someone he was going to do an act of charity. I didn't put it together as quick as I should have. I thought Ferguson was going to make some kind of play to draw me out in the open. But I figured he was going after your father. That's why I came over here to the doc's."

"Really?"

"Really. Now, calm down. We'll sort this out. I think Ferguson and the Tollivers are trying to bring things to a head. They seem pretty desperate. But giving myself up won't solve anything. They'll win that battle, and you might lose everything."

"What do you mean?" she asked.

"I mean, even if you exchanged me for Charity, I'll bet dollars to bear claws that the Tollivers would keep Charity for a bargaining chip in this high-stakes poker game."

"You're smarter than you look, Slocum."

"Let's go back to your office and think all this out. I'm sure I can come up with a plan that will get your sister back safely and put the Tollivers in their place."

"Do you really think you can get Charity back?"

"Sure," Slocum said, but he knew he was lying through his teeth. Still, he did need time to think. Ferguson held all the cards at the moment, and the Tollivers were backing him, that was sure. It looked to Slocum as if the Tollivers were growing impatient. They wanted something and were willing to go to any lengths to get it. They'd already resorted to murder, and now they had added a kidnapping to their stacked deck.

Lurlene rode a different way back to the office,

taking side streets instead of the main road through town. The streets were sparsely populated, largely undeveloped, and the two riders made good time. Slocum noticed that Lurlene was a good rider, was comfortable on her horse and in command.

Lenny was sitting in the office, holding a bloody cloth to his head. The yards were full of wagons, and men were shouting and cursing out back. Lenny was checking over the papers that were stacked in front of him on the desk where Charity usually sat.

"Sis, we're loaded up here," he said. "Did you find Charity?"

"No, of course not. All I've got is Slocum here."

Lenny looked sheepish. He avoided looking at Slocum, and tipped his head down and buried his nose back in his work. Lurlene snorted at her brother and stormed past him into her father's office. As soon as Slocum entered, she slammed the door shut behind him.

"Now, Slocum," she said, "you'd better come up with some damned good answers and a plan for getting my sister back or—"

Slocum didn't wait for her to finish, but grabbed both her arms and pulled her toward him. He held her tightly as she struggled to free her arms.

"Now, you listen to me, young lady. I don't take orders from you and I'm fed up with your threats. So just shut up and get off your high horse. I'm not some lackey you can order around or strike matches on. Understand?"

"Take your hands off of me, Slocum," she said, her voice low and threatening.

Instead of obeying her order, Slocum pulled her even closer to him. Then he kissed her hard on her lips, and held the kiss until she stopped squirming.

When he broke the kiss, Lurlene went limp all over. He let her arms fall to her side and stared into her brown eyes.

"Wha—what did you do that for?" she gasped.

"It was better than putting a gag in your mouth."

"I—I think I'd prefer the gag."

"And maybe I just wanted to see if there was a woman behind that tough bitch that keeps barking at me."

"Well, did you?" Her tone was taunting.

"Did I what?"

"Did you find a woman under that kiss?"

"Maybe. I haven't decided yet. Look, can we start all over? I know this is a serious situation, but I didn't cause it and I think maybe I can resolve it."

"I'm listening."

"Sit down then," Slocum said.

Lurlene hesitated, as if unwilling to take orders from Slocum. But a look into his eyes changed her mind and she walked meekly to her father's chair and sat down behind his desk. Slocum sat in the chair facing her.

"Now, Lurlene, the way I figure it is like this. Ferguson is desperate. He was supposed to get me out of the way. He and Jasper Tolliver were sent after me to do that. It didn't work, and he's in trouble with the Tollivers. He's desperate, so he kidnapped your sister, hoping to draw me out in the open."

"So what? This doesn't get my sister back safe and sound."

"If you start playing Ferguson's game, you've lost before you even start."

"So what do we do?"

"Charity is Ferguson's ace in the hole. He either thinks you'll deliver me to Tolliver or I'll do the decent thing and give myself up."

"But neither is going to happen, right?"

"Not if you want to beat Ferguson and the Tollivers. He's not going to hurt Charity. He's not going to kill her. If he does, he stands to lose, and he's probably a man who doesn't like to lose and probably is not used to losing."

"I think you have Ferguson pegged right, John. As far as it goes. But he's mean and he's a killer. And he's got my sister."

"What I think you can do is stall the Tollivers until tonight. Tell them you're going to bring me in tomorrow. I know where Ferguson stays when he's in town. I'll go after him, and if he's got your sister with him, I'll get her back for you."

"That sounds risky to me," she said. "Why should the Tolliver bunch believe me?"

"They have no other choice. Ferguson wants me and he'll have to go along with your story."

"I hope you're right."

"There are no Tollivers in Harrison, right?"

"As far as I know. They have a man in charge at their yard here, but he's no kin to the Tollivers."

"Then this man and whoever works for him don't have much of a stake in this situation. They're not going to look for trouble. They just want jobs and their pay every week."

"Yes, I think you're right."

"So, all we have to deal with is Ferguson, and he's way out on a limb here. By now, he knows I'm not an easy target. He'll be on his guard, but I'll find him and I'll put him to the wall."

"When?"

"By tonight, I hope."

"If my sister is not back home safe and sound by tomorrow morning, Slocum, I'll put *you* to the wall." Lurlene's eyes told Slocum she was serious. Dead serious.

He arose from his chair.

"I'll get her back, Lurlene," he said. "Or die trying."

16

The day was long in the tooth by the time Slocum rode back up to The Razorback saloon. He rode the back way he had learned from Lurlene so that he wouldn't attract undue attention or give any indication of where he was going to anyone who might be watching for him.

He did not go through the town square, but came into the main part of town from the creek side, and rode the back alley to a place within walking distance of the saloon. There were horses tied up outside, but none, he noted, at the house where Kitty had said Ferguson lived. But he hadn't expected it would be easy to find the outlaw.

Slocum walked into the saloon quickly, ready to draw if anyone challenged him. No one did. He saw Kitty sitting at the same place at the bar, and walked over to a table nearby and sat down, facing the door.

"Kentucky whiskey," he said to the bartender. "And Kitty, I'll buy your next drink when you're ready."

"I'm always ready, honey," she said, flashing a gap-toothed grin at Slocum. She slid off the bar stool, sidled over to his table, and sat down, scooting her chair close to his. At least, he thought, she didn't block his view. Her breath reeked of cheap whiskey, and he knew she was three sheets to the wind.

"Did I miss anything?" Slocum asked after the barkeep set a bottle in front of Slocum and picked up the ten-dollar bill that was already there.

"Same old bunch," she said.

"You haven't seen Pete Ferguson?"

"Well, I saw him, but he wasn't here very long. He come in with two fellers. They had one drink apiece and then left."

Slocum tried to act as if he was not very interested. "Oh? Do you know who the other two fellers were?"

"You bet. I've seen them in here before. Not often, mind you, but every so often. One of 'em's named Karl, the other's named Ivan. They own a freight outfit here in town. Tolliver's."

Slocum felt the hackles rise on the back of his neck. If the Tollivers were in town, that would explain why Ferguson was trying to bring things to a head. All of this must have been planned long in advance for the Tollivers to be in Harrison so soon after Slocum's arrival.

"Do you know where the Tollivers stay when they're in town?" Slocum asked.

"Do you know the road to Lead Hill?"

"No," Slocum said.

"You go past the cemetery north. The Tollivers

have got 'em a spread just north of town on the Lead Hill road. You can't miss it. It's a big old house and it's right off the road. They don't stay there much, but they got a woman out there who keeps it for them."

"A woman?"

"Oh, that was quite a scandal here in town a few years back. Nobody knows the whole story, but rumor has it that this woman was cheatin' on her husband with Karl Tolliver. She had a kid by him and when her husband found out, he kicked her out, but kept the kid. The woman moved out to the Tolliver place. When she comes into town, she's always dressed in mourning clothes."

"Do you know who the woman is?"

"This happened ten, twelve years ago. The talk died down quick, though, because nobody wanted to admit that such a scandal could happen in nice old proper Harrison. That woman always wears a veil, like she's just come from a funeral. Never shows her face. Always dressed in black."

"Somebody here in town must know who she is," Slocum said.

"Doc Leeds delivered her baby, which wasn't her husband's kid. He knows who she is because he goes out there to the Tollivers' once a month to see the lady."

"Why?"

"They say the lady has got sick over the years and Doc Leeds takes care of her."

"Thanks, Kitty. You've been a big help."

"Ain't nobody goin' to talk about this to a

stranger, John. If I wasn't likkered up, I wouldn't talk about it. It's kind of like a town secret, you know?"

"Yeah," Slocum said. "I know. Every family has skeletons in its closet, and towns are no different."

Kitty laughed. She had been talking in low tones, almost in a whisper, and her laughter was loud, and caused some of the patrons to look over at her and Slocum.

"Finish the bottle, Kitty," Slocum said. "It's paid for. But take care of yourself."

"Oh, I always take care of myself. If you ever get lonesome . . ."

"I'll look you up," Slocum said.

Slocum rode through the twilight to Doc Leeds's house. Lamps were lit in most of the houses, and Doc's place was more brightly lit than any of them. When Slocum walked into the parlor, it was empty.

"Doc," Slocum called. "Are you here?"

The nurse came out. "Is this an emergency?" she said. "Oh, it's you. What do you want? Dr. Leeds is closing his offices for the day."

"I need to talk to him for a few minutes."

"He's with Mr. Barnes. Could you come back to-morrow?"

"No, it's important I see Dr. Leeds right now. And if Mr. Barnes doesn't mind, I'd like to see him too."

"Just a minute."

The nurse was back within moments.

"Come with me," she said.

Leeds and Barnes were in a bedroom that had been converted into a hospital room. Chad was lying in bed, a large pillow under his buttocks. Leeds sat in a chair at his bedside with a stethoscope, listening to Barnes's heartbeat. He removed the stethoscope from his ears and let it dangle around his neck.

"Chad's doing fine, Mr. Slocum. We're just thinking about supper." The doctor appeared to be perturbed over Slocum's intrusion.

"This won't take long, Doc. I need some information."

"You didn't come to see Chad?"

"Well, yes, and you too."

Both men looked at Slocum with apprehension. The doctor cleared his throat and looked at his nurse. "You can go home, Earlene. Tell Mrs. Briggs I'll be ready to eat in thirty minutes. She can bring Mr. Barnes's plate in here too."

"Good night, Doctor."

"Close the door, will you, Earlene?"

The nurse left, closing the door behind her.

"Now what is this all about, Mr. Slocum?" Leeds asked.

"I smell something fishy here, with the kidnapping of Charity and some other things I've come across down here."

Slocum watched the faces of both Leeds and Barnes. He saw the blood drain from the cheeks of both men.

"Fishy?" Leeds asked.

"When I was in the Barnes house, I saw no pictures of his wife, nor have I heard any mention of a Mrs. Barnes. That seems peculiar enough."

"My wife died a long time ago," Barnes said.

"I don't think so, Chad. The only thing Charity has in common with either her brother, Lenny, or her sister, Lurlene, is her brown eyes."

"What are you driving at, Mr. Slocum?" Leeds asked.

"I haven't got it all pieced together yet, Doc, but maybe you will be good enough to tell me if the woman you tend to at the Tolliver house is Mrs. Chad Barnes."

Barnes let out a low curse. The doctor's facial muscles tightened up as if he had been splashed with hot water. His lips pursed in anger, and he looked as if he was going to explode.

"You've got a nerve," Dr. Leeds said. "My patients are none of your business."

"I think this one is. I think that woman had an illegitimate daughter named Charity. And I think one of the Tollivers, Karl maybe, or Ivan, is Charity's father."

"Slocum," Barnes said, "you are one pure sonofabitch, you know that? And you're full of shit to boot."

"Am I? Well, if I'm wrong, I apologize. But I don't think Charity was kidnapped at all. I think Pete Ferguson just took her out to her mother's place to try and draw me out so he could kill me."

"Maybe you'd better go on back to Springfield, Slocum," Barnes said. "You're in way over your head."

"No, Chad, I tell you what I'm going to do. I'm going to go out there to the Tolliver house and see if Charity is there with her mother."

"Damn you, Slocum," Barnes said. "Stay the hell out of my business."

"Did you know Karl and Ivan Tolliver were in town?"

Neither man answered. Barnes looked as if he'd been kicked in the groin, and Dr. Leeds grew red in the face.

"Well, they are, and I think they mean to take over your freight business by force. I think they're tired of waiting. And with me in the picture, they know it's time for a showdown."

"You—you'll get killed if you go out there," Dr. Leeds said. "Ferguson is just waiting for you to show up."

"I figured you might know that, Doc. When I finish up out there I'm going to ask Lurlene if she knows the true story of her family."

"Damn you, Slocum," Barnes shouted. "You keep your damned mouth shut to Lurlene."

Slocum knew he had struck a nerve. He had gone way out on a limb with his theory, but it was the only one that made sense to him. There was too much lying, too much secrecy, too much deception among the Barnes family members and their doctor. And Charity's kidnapping was just too neat and bloodless. Tolliver had some kind of hold over Barnes, and maybe he had wanted to take over the Barnes freight company for a long time. Maybe

Chad's wife had been the one to push Tolliver into making his moves.

"Doc, Chad," Slocum said. "I'll be seeing you."

"No, wait," Dr. Leeds said. "Don't go out there to Tolliver's."

"Why? Are you afraid I'll find out that I'm right? That I'll find out the truth about Charity and her mother?"

"Let him go, Harvey," Barnes said. "He's going to find out anyway."

Barnes seemed resigned to what Slocum was going to do. He wore a hangdog look on his face, the look of a beaten man.

"No, Estelle is my patient," said Leeds. "She's not well. I won't have Slocum barging in on her like this."

"Estelle? Is that your wife's name, Chad?" Slocum asked.

Barnes said nothing, but Slocum knew the answer anyway.

He left the two men without another word. He saw them exchange glances, and then Barnes closed his eyes and lay back on his pillow as if all the life had been taken from him.

As Slocum walked out of the doctor's house, he made another decision. He would go to the Tolliver house, all right, but he wanted witnesses. There was one more stop he wanted to make before he rode out there. If his hunch was right, neither Lurlene nor Lenny knew the truth about their mother and their little sister, Charity.

He hoped he could convince them that family secrets could be dangerous and very destructive. Their father, Chad, had kept this one for far too long.

17

The Barnes house was dark except for a lamp in the living room when Slocum arrived. It looked as if Lurlene had just arrived, because her horse was still tied up outside at the hitch rail. And when he had passed the freight office, it had been dark. He wondered where Lenny was.

"John?" Lurlene called out as Slocum crossed the porch, his boots pounding on the hardwoods.

"Yes, it's me."

"Come in. Do you have news for me?"

"Where's Lenny?" he asked as he entered the room. Lurlene was not there, but was talking to him from either the hall or another room.

"Lenny? Why, he went into town after he closed the office. He went to see Daddy and then he was going out with some of the boys who work for us. I don't expect him until late. Why do you ask?"

Slocum was about to reply when Lurlene walked into the room, fluffing her hair. She was wearing a light housecoat and from what he could see, nothing else whatsoever. She was barefoot and the housecoat was not fastened tightly, so that when she walked, her long legs flashed with each step.

"What's the matter with you?" she asked. "Cat got your tongue?"

"No, I, uh, I just wasn't expecting you to be, ah, well, so comfortable."

Lurlene laughed. "I was just going to pour myself some whiskey. It's been a long, taxing day. Would you like some, John?"

"I, uh, if you have Kentucky bourbon, I might have a taste."

"We've got Old Taylor, Daddy's favorite. That's what I was going to pour. Do you like it mixed with branch water?"

"No, straight is fine," he said. He watched as Lurlene slinked to a hand-carved bar at the far end of the room. She walked behind it and he heard the clink of glasses, the clank of bottles. She set out two tumblers and poured each of them nearly full. Then she glided around the bar with the filled glasses in her hands and came up to him, holding one glass out for him.

"Thanks," he said.

"I was just going to take a bath," she said. "I'm having Betsy draw me a hot one. There's a little room in back of the kitchen where I bathe."

"Don't let me keep you," he said.

"I don't like the water too hot, and Betsy makes it scalding. There's no hurry. It will take her a while to fill the tub, and more time to let the water cool some. Let's sit on the divan and be comfortable, shall we? Then you can tell me what you've been doing to get my sister back. To tell you the truth, I'm disappointed that she's not with you."

"Are you still mad at me?" Slocum asked as the two of them sat down on the divan.

"Yes. But all afternoon, I've been thinking of that kiss. My lips are still burning."

"Maybe the drink will take away the sting, Lurlene."

"Oh, the kiss doesn't sting, but it went deep. I've never been kissed by a man like that. Not ever. You caught me quite by surprise."

"Perhaps I took liberties I shouldn't have, but you were raking me pretty good with your tongue."

She crossed her legs and her frock fell away, displaying a pair of bare legs. The gesture was not lost on Slocum, but he took a sip of the whiskey to quench the fires that were starting to kindle in his loins.

"My tongue has other purposes besides talking," she said.

"I'm sure it does."

"Now, what about Charity? Do you know where she is? Is she safe?"

"I have a pretty good idea where she is, and yes, I think she's safe. I still have a few questions, though, mainly for you."

"For me?"

"Yes, I want to know about your mother, Lurlene."

Lurlene was taking a sip of whiskey, and nearly

choked at the question. She cleared her throat and drew in a deep breath.

"What's my mother have to do with this?"

"Maybe nothing. Maybe everything."

"My mother died shortly after Charity was born. A long time ago."

"You knew her then?"

"I knew her, of course. Daddy said she took sick at the hospital."

"So you raised Charity," Slocum said.

"Well, she had a nanny. Lenny and I were in school."

"Why are there no pictures of your mother or her family in this house?"

"Daddy said, well, he was broken up pretty bad when our mother passed away. He said he couldn't stand to have reminders of her. I don't know what he did with all the pictures."

"Have you seen any of your mother's family since she died?"

"No. Her family was from Tennessee. I guess we lost touch with them. John, why are you asking all these questions about my mother? I haven't thought of her in years."

"I guess I'm just curious. Your daddy didn't mention your mother and neither did you or Lenny. Pardon me for prying."

"No, John, you have a reason for asking about my mother. It's not just idle curiosity."

"No, it's not. But I can't tell you any more right now. By tomorrow, I should be able to tell you everything. And you'll have your sister back."

"If you know where she is, why don't you just go and get her? Are you afraid of Ferguson?"

"It's not just Ferguson now."

"What do you mean?"

"The Tollivers blew into town today. Karl and Ivan."

Lurlene reared back on the divan, shock registering on her face.

"That's unusual," she said. "For both of them to come to Harrison at once."

"It looks like they're going to put more pressure on your daddy to sell them his business."

"Well, he never will."

"No, I expect not."

Lurlene turned pensive. Her forehead wrinkled in thought. "But of course, now that they have Charity . . ."

"They won't have her for long."

"You sound pretty sure of yourself."

"I have some details to work out."

"Can you share those with me, John?"

"I'm still working on them."

"Good. Then we have time."

"Time?"

"I want to see if you kiss that way all the time."

"All the time?" Slocum chewed on his drink, wondering what Lurlene had on her mind.

She set her drink down and took his from his hand. She moved closer to him, squirming next to his body. She put a hand in his lap, and began to explore what was inside his trousers.

"Why don't you take off that frock coat?" she asked.

"I wasn't going to stay long."

"You can always put it back on when you're ready to leave. Here, I'll help you."

She helped him take off his coat, and draped it over the end of the divan. "And your pistol." She began unbuckling his gunbelt.

"Lurlene, better be careful," he said. "You might get into something you can't get out of easily."

"Maybe I want to," she purred, putting her lips on his neck while her hand groped at his groin again. "Oh, there he is," she said. "Growing nicely."

"Are you sure about this?" he asked.

She nibbled at his neck, and Slocum felt the hairs stiffen at the base of his skull. "Umm," she said, and he felt her tongue lave his skin like a hot caress.

"Lurlene, you're starting something."

"I know," she breathed, and her fingers worked at the buttons of his fly. Then her hand was inside, grasping, probing, finding his manhood, clasping it tightly while her lips moved up his neck to his chin and then over to his mouth.

She kissed him and squeezed his prick. He leaned over and slid his hands inside her housecoat, and felt her soft breasts beneath, soft and firm, the nipples beginning to stand up like buttons.

"Ummm," she moaned. "Yes, that feels nice."

"Don't you think we ought to move out of the living room, or at least blow out the lamp?" he asked, the heat in his loins spreading through his body like a flowing river of lava.

"John, I'm so hot," she said, her breath hot in his ear. "Let's go upstairs, quick."

"Yeah, we'd better. We wouldn't want Mrs. Pritchett walking in here right now."

"Hurry," she said, breaking her embrace. Slocum grabbed his gunbelt, and followed her up the stairs and down the hall to her room. It was dark, and she didn't light a lamp. He heard a rustling sound as she took off her housecoat, and then the bedsprings creaked as she put her weight on the bed.

Slocum put his gunbelt down next to the bed within easy reach, sat down and took off his boots, then stripped out of his pants and shirt. When he lay down next to her, she was waiting for him, her arms open, her kisses peppering his face with an eagerness that surprised him.

She reached down to his loin and grasped his prick in her hand and squeezed it. He cupped her cunt and plied it with a single finger until she squirmed as if skewered on a spit. She was wet inside and she pulled him on top of her, begging him to take her. He lowered himself and plunged inside her. She cried out with joy, and her hips began to move up and down in the ancient rhythm of lovemaking.

"Yes, John, yes," she cried. "It's so good. Take me, take me."

He pumped his prick back and forth in the velvet folds of her cunt while she squirmed and bucked with pleasure.

Slocum took her to the heights and back as the bedsprings creaked under the strain of their romping bodies. Finally, in a last surge of energy, she held on to his buttocks and he exploded his balls inside her. She screamed softly and gasped as she climaxed in the same moment. Then she let out a long sigh of delight, and squeezed his buttocks until they were bloodless where her fingers dug into his flesh.

"Oh, John, that was wonderful," she sighed. "That first kiss of yours was a promise and you filled that promise. Thank you."

"Thank you," he said, and lay atop her, heaving until he could regain his breath.

They both heard a noise at the door as it swung wide.

"Slocum, I'm going to kill you, you bastard."

Then they both heard the ominous click of a pistol hammer cocking back. Lurlene screamed into the deadly silence of the room.

18

Slocum dove over the side of the bed and snatched his Colt from its holster. He rolled to one side, cocking the pistol. He saw the dark silhouette in the doorway, but could not see who it was.

"John, don't," Lurlene screamed. "It's Lenny."

"Where is that bastard?" Lenny asked, stepping out of the doorway and into the darkened room.

"Lenny, don't," Lurlene pleaded. "Don't shoot."

"Sis, you don't know anything about this. I'm going to kill that bastard Slocum. Where is he?"

"If you pull that trigger, Lenny," Slocum said. "I'll blow you to hell."

As soon as he spoke, Slocum crabbed away from where he was sprawled on the floor. He saw Lenny swing his pistol to aim it at him. Slocum gathered his legs under him and sprang forward, toward Lenny, keeping low.

Before Lenny could fire, Slocum slammed into his knees, bowling him over. Lenny's pistol went off with a loud roar. Smoke and sparks spewed from the barrel, but the bullet smashed into the ceiling overhead.

Lenny went down, with Slocum atop him. Slocum grabbed Lenny's pistol and laid the barrel hard against the side of Lenny's head. Behind him, Slocum heard Lurlene scramble out of the bed.

She went to a small table, struck a match, and lit the lamp. Slocum held Lenny's arms down, pinning him to the floor. Slocum slowly let the hammer down on his pistol, left it at half-cock.

In seconds, the lamp flickered and Lurlene turned the wick up, filling the room with light.

"Don't hurt him, John," she said.

"Get off me, Slocum," Lenny snarled.

"I don't like this any better than you do, Lenny. Just behave yourself, or I'll knock you out cold."

Lurlene walked over, her naked body silhouetted in the lamp glow.

"You both look ridiculous," she said.

Slocum released his grip on Lenny's arms and stood up, holding both pistols. Lenny lay there, face-up, dazed, his face contorted in anger.

"You can get up, Lenny," Slocum said.

Lenny struggled to his feet, then stood there on wobbly legs, holding his head with one hand on the spot where Slocum had struck him. He fixed his gaze on Slocum, glared at him.

"Now, Lenny," Slocum said, "take a deep breath and tell me why you wanted to shoot me."

Lenny looked at his sister. "I—I went to see Daddy and he told me Slocum had been to see him.

He told me to be careful and to stay away from him."

"So that's why you tried to kill John?" Lurlene asked.

"No, it was what Doc Leeds told me that got me riled up."

"And what did the good doctor tell you, Lenny?" Slocum asked, edging toward the bed to retrieve his clothes.

"Dr. Leeds said you was trying to destroy our family. He said that you had kidnapped Charity and raped her, and were probably at my house raping—you, Lurlene. So when I saw his horse outside, I got burned and come up here. I figured what Doc Leeds had told me was right, that you was being raped by this bastard here."

"Doc Leeds is a liar," Slocum said.

"Then what was you doin' here with my sister, you bastard?"

"I wasn't raping her," Slocum said.

"He wasn't raping me, Lenny," Lurlene said, her voice very soft and calm. "And John didn't kidnap Charity. You know that. It was Ferguson who knocked you out cold, wasn't it?"

"Yes, that's true," Lenny said. "But Doc Leeds said Slocum was in cahoots with the Tollivers and with Pete Ferguson."

"I repeat," Slocum said, "Doc Leeds is a liar. But I can understand why he lied to you."

"Then you tell me, Slocum."

"Let me get dressed. Then I want you and Lurlene

both to come with me. We're going to take a little ride."

Lurlene shot a glance at Slocum, a questioning look in her eyes.

"Where to?" Lenny asked.

"I'll tell you on the way. Now back on out of here while I get some clothes on. Go saddle Lurlene's horse and meet us out in front of the house."

"Sis?" Lenny looked at Lurlene.

"Do what he says, Lenny. I'll be out in a minute. Tell Betsy we'll be home later. She can stop drawing my bath."

Lenny nodded and left the room. Slocum threw both pistols on the bed and started putting his shirt and pants back on.

"What's this all about, John?" Lurlene asked, gliding to the wardrobe in the center of one wall.

"I'm still trying to put it all together myself, but as I told Lenny, I'll tell you both what I think when we go where I'm taking you both."

"You're a man of mystery, John."

Slocum grinned. He strapped on his gunbelt, slid his hideout pistol in under his shirt back of the buckle, and tucked Lenny's pistol in his waistband. He watched as Lurlene donned a pair of black riding pants and a black blouse, then pulled on her riding boots. She combed her hair quickly as Slocum watched her with a look of wonder in his eyes.

"The lady in black," he said.

"I was told my mother was fond of wearing black clothes. I guess I inherited her taste. By the way, I'm going to take a pistol with me when we leave."

"Do you shoot a pistol?"

"I'm a crack shot," she said. "And so is Lenny. You're lucky, John, he couldn't see you in the dark."

Slocum swallowed, and a shiver ran up his spine. It had been a close call at that, he thought. "Ready?" he asked, striding toward the door.

"Yes, my pistol and gunbelt are downstairs in the gun cabinet. Our father taught us both to shoot and hunt. Did you know that?"

"Your father is the real man of mystery here," Slocum said. "No, I didn't know that."

"Every fall the three of us hunt deer and turkey."

"What about Charity?" Slocum asked. "Didn't your daddy teach her to shoot and hunt?"

The two of them walked out the door and down the stairs to the living room.

"No, for some reason he wanted Charity to grow up and be a lady of refinement. Or so he said. I think Charity resented it when the three of us went hunting while Daddy sent her off to Little Rock to stay with his sister."

"So your daddy treated Charity different than you and Lenny?"

"Yes. How did you know?"

"I didn't. But I'm curious about her. Did you and Lenny treat her any different?"

Lurlene opened the gun cabinet in a closet in the downstairs hallway. There were rifles and shotguns and pistols, some on display, some in holsters. It was a large cabinet. She slipped a gunbelt off one of the dowels set in the wall. She strapped the belt on, pulled the pistol, checked the cylinders. It was a

Smith & Wesson .38, with the crack-top barrel, and it was fully loaded. The gunbelt glistened with .38 cartridges. She put the pistol back in its holster, which was finely made of hand-tooled leather.

"What do you mean?" she asked, closing the closet.

"I mean did you and Lenny treat her differently than you treated each other?"

"I don't think so. Lenny and I were older, though, and we had different interests. I suppose Charity, being the youngest, the baby of the family, might have felt left out of some things."

"Some things?"

"Well, Daddy never took her hunting or showed her how to shoot. And he never let her ride a horse, so she stayed at home when Lenny and I went riding."

They walked together to the living room. Betsy met them on the way.

"Lenny says you'll not be takin' your bath now, Miss Lurlene."

"No, later, Betsy. Sorry."

"Well, you come and get me when you're ready, hear?"

"I will. Good night, Betsy."

Betsy, a gray-haired, subdued lady, gave a weak smile and tottered off to the kitchen on spindly legs. She was very thin, and her gray hair was put up in a bun. Slocum thought she could have been anywhere from forty to sixty years of age. It was hard to tell.

Slocum and Lurlene walked out on the porch to

wait for Lenny to show up with their horses. The Arabian whickered when it saw Slocum.

"So Charity more or less grew up by herself," Slocum said.

"No, we took her buggy riding and on picnics. What are you asking all these questions about Charity for, John?"

"I'm just curious."

But it was all beginning to make sense to Slocum. Chad Barnes had treated Charity differently than he had treated Lenny and Lurlene. Maybe he hadn't meant to, but he had. And if Slocum's hunch was right, that Chad wasn't her father, then it all made sense. A lot of things were starting to make sense. He just wondered how Lurlene and Lenny would take it once they found out the truth about their mother, their sister, and their father.

It was a bridge he had to cross.

And he meant to cross it very soon.

19

Slocum handed Lenny's pistol over to him.

"You might need this where we're going, Lenny."

"Where are we going?"

Slocum and Lurlene climbed onto their horses.

"We're going to see some people," Slocum said. "Do either of you know the road to Lead Hill?"

"We know it," Lurlene said.

"Then let's go. Lead the way."

"Are you going out to the Tolliver place?" Lurlene asked as they rode down toward the freight office and the main road.

"Do you know the place?" Slocum asked.

"Yes, we've seen it a couple of times. Daddy doesn't like us to ride out that way, though. He says it's a dangerous road. Lead Hill is a mining town and there are some roughnecks out that way."

"I think your daddy's right, Lurlene. There probably are some roughnecks out that way."

They rode in silence for a time, as if each was thinking of the journey out of town that night. Slocum was sure that Lurlene and Lenny were thinking up all sorts of questions to ask. But he knew he had gotten their interest, and knew they were both more than just passingly curious about where they were going.

"When are you going to tell us where we're going and why?" Lurlene asked as they turned onto the Lead Hill road, passing the town cemetery, which was dark and silent.

"Now is as good a time as any, I guess."

"We *are* going to the Tolliver place, aren't we?" Lenny said.

"It could get dangerous," Slocum said. "Both Karl and Ivan Tolliver are in town, and I'm betting they're at their house."

"The Tollivers are in town?" Lurlene exclaimed. "Why on earth would we want to go out there? They're the scoundrels who are trying to run Linda out of business and take over Daddy's freight yard."

"That's what's been so puzzling about all this treachery and double-dealing," Slocum said. "Apparently, the Tollivers have wanted your daddy's business for a long time, and then they saw a way to get it all. Drive Linda Collins out of business and take over that line and yours. So they arranged to kill Ralph Collins. Probably hired Ferguson to gun Collins down. They probably thought that would leave the way clear to move in and take over from Linda and then go after your daddy."

"But Linda hired you," Lurlene said. "And that probably made Karl Tolliver mad as hell."

"Oh, I'm sure I'm the fly in the ointment, all right.

But the Tollivers have wanted all the freight business for some time. All of this that happened in the past couple of days is just the result of the greed that's been brewing for some time."

"It's true," Lenny said. "Karl has made Daddy an offer several times to buy us out."

"Did your daddy ever tell you why he wouldn't sell out to Tolliver? It would have been the easy path to take."

"No, he never did," Lurlene said. "He just said he'd never sell to Karl Tolliver, and told us that if anything ever happened to him, to hold onto the business and never sell out to Karl Tolliver."

"Did you ever wonder why your daddy was so against selling out to Tolliver?"

"No, we just thought he didn't like the Tollivers."

"But you never asked why he hated them so much?"

"We didn't ask him why, but we wondered about it."

"Good," Slocum said, "because there's a reason for everything."

"What are you getting at, John?" Lurlene asked.

"Family secrets maybe."

The town began to thin out as they rode into farming and cattle country. The lights of Harrison disappeared in their wake as they rode over low rolling hills smelling of hay and corn and wheat. It was good country, Slocum thought, reminding him a little of his native Georgia, the scents bringing with them a touch of sadness and nostalgia.

Lamplight glowed in some of the scattered farmhouses, looking like distant stars on the horizon. None of the houses were large. They were simple frame dwellings, practical and functional, with large barns and outbuildings that were now dark.

"The Tolliver house is about two miles from here," Lurlene said. "It'll be on our left. You can't miss it."

"Good," Slocum said.

"You still haven't told us why we're going out there at this time of night, John." Lurlene rode alongside him, while Lenny rode a few yards ahead of them.

"For one thing, I believe your sister Charity is there."

"A prisoner."

"Maybe. Maybe not."

"What in hell does that mean?"

"I believe her kidnapping was more or less a fake."

"A fake?"

"Ferguson knocked out your brother to make it look like a kidnapping, but I think Charity went with him willingly out there."

"Why do you think that?"

"It has to do with those family secrets I mentioned."

"I don't understand," she said.

"Maybe you will when we get there."

"I think you owe Lenny and me an explanation before we get there."

"All right. I do. Let's stop when we see the Tolliver place and I'll fill you in on my thinking, see if any of it makes sense to you."

"I think you'd better, John. I don't like mysteries."

They were silent for a time, and then Lenny reined his horse up.

"Yonder is the Tolliver place, Slocum," he said. "And somebody's home. They have lamps lit downstairs."

Slocum and Lurlene pulled up to a stop. Slocum looked at the large house. It was not a mansion such as those owned by the plantation owners in Georgia, but it was an imposing presence on the plain as it sat on a small knoll, surrounded by box elders and walnut, oak, and willow trees. It was far larger than any of the other houses he'd seen.

"Well," Slocum said, "there it is. I wonder what kind of a welcome we'll get there."

"Not much," Lenny said. "The Tollivers are our enemies, and if they've got Charity . . ."

"Oh, I think Charity is there," Slocum said. "And she probably won't be glad to see us either."

"Of course she will," Lurlene said. "She's our sister. She's family."

"When we get there," Slocum said, "I'm going to make certain accusations. Then you can judge for yourself how much of a sister Charity is to you."

Lenny drew his pistol, leveled it at Slocum.

"I've had enough of you, Slocum. What accusations? You better not be accusing Charity of nothing."

"It's about time you opened your eyes, Lenny,"

Slocum said. "Put that pistol back in its holster and listen. Maybe it will all make sense to you."

"Do what he says, Lenny," Lurlene said. "We can't go up there if we're fighting among ourselves."

Reluctantly, Lenny slid his pistol back in its holster.

"Well, you'd better talk then, Slocum, and you'd better talk damned fast," Lenny said.

"First of all"—Slocum drew in a breath, then let it out as he spoke—"I think your mother is alive and living in that house up there. If I'm right, we should see Doc Leeds there. Do you know his horse?"

Both Lenny and Lurlene nodded.

"I think she's probably ill and Doc Leeds has been taking care of her. He certainly has been keeping her secret."

"You can't be right about that, John," Lurlene said. "Our mother's dead. Daddy told us so. He was stricken with grief when she died."

"Here's what I think happened," Slocum said. "I think your mother had an affair with Karl Tolliver, or maybe with Ivan. But I'll bet on Karl. I think he planned it that way a long time ago when it happened. I think he got your mother pregnant, and it was Charity who was born to her. I think your father found out that she was not his daughter—I don't know, maybe your mother told him, but my bet is that Karl Tolliver gloated about it and was the one who told him."

Both Lurlene and Lenny gasped.

"Slocum, you're a damned liar," Lenny said.

"I think your father kicked your mother out, or else Tolliver took her away and, to hide his shame, your father told you she had died. But he knows she's alive. I went to see him and Doc Leeds, and they told me to stay out of it."

"Damn you, Slocum," Lenny said. "You should have listened to our daddy."

"I think Charity has strong ties to Tolliver and her mother, and I think she's the one who told Ferguson when and how Ralph Collins was traveling to Springfield so that he could be waiting for him and kill him."

"Oh, no," Lurlene said. "Charity would never do such a despicable thing. You're practically accusing her of murder."

"Charity may not have known that Ferguson was going to kill Collins. My guess is once she found out, she confronted her father, or ran to her mother and told her she didn't want any part of their scheme to take your daddy's business away from him. She must bear a certain fondness for Chad since he raised her."

"This is all unthinkable, John," Lurlene said.

"It may be unthinkable, but I think you're going to find out that I'm right in a few minutes. You'll be able to see it on Charity's face and on her mother's. Do you remember your mother?"

"A little," Lenny said. "I think."

"I remember her," Lurlene said, "but that was so long ago and her image has faded in my memory some. She'll—if she's alive, as you say—she'll look different."

"I'm sure she will. But you'll know if that's your mother in there. I'm sure of that."

"What if Tolliver raises hell about us coming to his house and you making all these accusations?" Lenny asked. "He might want to shoot you."

"He might want to shoot us all," Lurlene said.

"It's not Tolliver I'm worried about," Slocum said. "It's Pete Ferguson. If he's there, and he probably is, he's the one who'll try and gun me down."

"John, I don't think we'd better go up there," Lurlene said. "It's just too dangerous. And if you're wrong about all this, it will just hurt Charity so much she'll want to die."

"It's too late to back out now," Slocum said. "I came here to do a job and I'm going to finish it. With or without you two."

Lurlene and Lenny looked at each other.

"He means it, Lenny," she said.

Lenny sighed deeply. "I guess we've got to know, don't we, sis?"

"Yes," she said. "We've got to know if our mother is still alive."

"And you've got to know what happened when Charity was born," Slocum said.

"God help us," Lurlene said, and it was almost like a prayer on her lips.

20

Lenny was the first to spot the horse at the hitch rall outside the Tolliver house.

"That's Doc Leeds's horse, Lurlene. Damn."

"It sure as hell is," Lurlene said, and Slocum could almost feel the anger building inside her.

"Let's be quiet," Slocum said. "We've got to get inside that house."

They rode up to the hitch rail quietly. Slocum kept his eyes on the windows, which were curtained, to see if anyone looked out. No one did.

He held his fingers to his lips as the three of them walked toward the porch. They all stepped lightly, and when they were at the door, Slocum looked at both of them to see if they were ready for what was going to happen next.

From inside, the murmur of voices seeped through the cracks in the front door.

"What are you going to do?" Lurlene whispered. "Go in, or knock?"

"I'm going in if the door isn't latched. Stay a few

steps behind me, in case there's any trouble."

The voices from inside grew louder, and Slocum waited.

"That's Doc Leeds," Lurlene whispered. "He's saying something about you, I think."

Slocum nodded. He had heard his name mentioned in angry tones.

Then they heard a woman's voice break in, high and shrill.

"That sounds like my mo—" Lurlene started to say.

Slocum pushed on the door. It gave way and swung open. They could all hear the voices from the front room very clearly as Slocum stepped gingerly inside, his right hand poised above his pistol. He had thought about bringing the Greener in, but had decided against it. He knew that would be seen as a hostile act by anyone inside, and could have opened the ball a lot sooner than he would have wished.

He tiptoed down the short hall. There was an open doorway to the right and the voices were emanating from there. Lamplight spilled through the opening. Beyond was an open foyer and another door on his left, which he thought might lead to the front dining room.

"Damn you, Pete, you should have put Slocum down when you had the chance."

Slocum didn't recognize the voice. He turned and looked at Lurlene. She formed two words with her lips. "Karl Tolliver," she said soundlessly.

Slocum nodded.

"That damned cafe was plumb full, Karl, and Slocum damned sure ain't no slouch with the Colt .44. He learned it good when he was with Quantrill."

"Shut up, both of you," a woman's voice said. "Harvey, you're going to have to help us."

"No, Estelle," Doc Leeds said. "I'm already in way over my head. I told you about Slocum and that's as far as I go here."

"Then we'll have to send Pete to your house to get rid of Chad. I've waited long enough. With Chad out of the way . . ."

"Mother, please, don't send Pete. I don't want you to kill my fath—to kill Chad."

Lurlene leaned close to Slocum and whispered in his ear. "Charity."

Slocum nodded.

"It has to be done," Estelle said. "Karl?"

"I reckon we better send Pete down to Doc's to finish off Chad," Tolliver said.

Slocum looked at Lenny, who was holding onto his sister, straining to hear every word. Slocum could see the anger suffuse his face, and he knew that Lenny was like a lit stick of dynamite. He could explode at any time.

He held up a hand to Lurlene and Lenny, and mouthed the word "Wait."

Then he walked to the doorway and entered a room that appeared to be a large parlor.

"It's Slocum," Ferguson exclaimed.

Every person in the room turned to face the intruder. Slocum quickly took in the situation. Two men were seated in large chairs. They were smoking

cigars. Charity and her mother stood in front of the
large divan. Doc Leeds was sitting in a chair near a
small desk. Pete Ferguson stood at the far end of
the room, a glass of whiskey in his hand, a cigarette
dangling from his lips.

They all looked like statues, or mannequins, fro-
zen in position. Slocum knew he had caught them
all totally by surprise.

"Ferguson," Slocum said, "if you go for that iron
on your hip, you're a dead man."

"Get him," Karl Tolliver said, rising from his
chair. "Estelle, put out the lamp."

At that moment, Lurlene and Lenny burst into the
room, their pistols drawn. Slocum heard them, but
did not look behind him. Instead, his eyes stayed on
Ferguson.

Estelle turned and started to walk toward the lamp
on the table near the divan. Ferguson's hand flew to
the butt of his pistol. His hand was a blur, and Slocum thought he was very fast.

But Slocum was faster. He drew his Colt and went
into a fighting crouch. His left hand knocked the
hammer back as the pistol emerged from his holster
and was cocked before he brought it level with Ferguson's midsection.

Ferguson's hand gripped the butt of his pistol, and
he had it halfway out of its holster when Slocum
squeezed the trigger of his Colt .44. The pistol
bucked in his hand, spewing out lead, flame, and
smoke.

Dr. Leeds ducked under the desk. Charity
screamed and put her hands up to her face. Ivan

Tolliver threw himself sideways. He and his chair crashed onto the carpeted floor. Karl Tolliver looked over at Ferguson, saw him crumple and shoot backward from the force of the bullet that tore through his gut with all the energy of a sixteen-pound sledgehammer.

Then Karl turned to look at Slocum. He half stood, and was reaching inside his shirt for something that Slocum took to be a hideout pistol.

Slocum swung the barrel of his Colt to come to bear on Karl Tolliver. Tolliver fished out a small pistol that had been tucked inside his waistband. Slocum fired at nearly point-blank range, and the bullet tore through Karl's hand and shattered the wooden butt of the pistol. Karl fell backward, a look of surprise on his face.

Estelle had started to turn down the wick on the lamp when Slocum walked over to her and pushed her away. Charity screamed in his ear.

Then Lurlene rushed up, grabbed her sister, and clamped a hand over her mouth. Lenny walked over to Ivan, who was trying to get back on his feet. Lenny aimed his pistol at Ivan's head.

"Just stay there, Ivan," Lenny said, "or I'll blow your damned head off, you bastard."

Ivan sat back down and stared into the ugly snout of Lenny's pistol.

Slocum heard a noise and knew what it was. He looked past Estelle and Lurlene and Charity and saw Ferguson sitting up, his pistol in his hand. The sound he had heard was that of Ferguson cocking his pistol.

"I should have—" Ferguson started to say, his quivering finger pulling on the trigger.

Slocum took deadly aim and fired at Ferguson. Ferguson's pistol exploded as his finger completed the squeeze. The shot went wild, but Slocum heard it smack into human flesh.

"Mother," Lurlene yelled.

Slocum turned and saw Estelle stagger toward him. Her hand fled to her side, and he saw blood pouring through a wound, soaking the black dress she wore. He grabbed her before she fell and laid her on the divan.

Estelle looked up at him, her eyes fiercely bright. Lurlene rushed over. So too did Lenny and Charity.

"Doc," Slocum said. "You'd better get over here and take a look at this woman."

"So you're Slocum," Estelle said. "You know you've spoiled everything."

"No, ma'am, you spoiled it. A long time ago."

"Oh, Mother," Charity pleaded, "please don't die."

Doc Leeds pushed everyone aside to look at Estelle. He knelt down beside her and held her hand.

"Harvey," she said.

"Don't try to talk. Let me see how bad it is," Leeds said.

"I know how bad it is, Harvey. I'm dying."

Charity started to cry. Lurlene put her arm around her sister. Lenny just stared down at the woman he now knew was his mother, a mother he had thought was dead.

Leeds felt around the wound in Estelle's side. Slocum stepped away, and walked to the far end of the room where Ferguson lay, mortally wounded.

"Slocum," Ferguson rasped.

"It had to come to this, Ferguson."

"Did you—did you buy them horses?"

Slocum smiled.

"I told you not to go look at 'em. I warned you."

"Yes, you did, Ferguson. Sometimes I don't listen real good."

Ferguson opened his mouth to say something else, but no words came out. He made a gurgling sound in his throat, and then his frosty eyes closed and he let out a last gasp of breath.

Karl Tolliver was dying. Ivan was still shaking. He had his face covered with both hands as if he was trying to hide or keep someone from sending a bullet into his brain.

"You can get up, Tolliver. I'm going to take you into Harrison and turn you over to the law."

"You ain't goin' to shoot me?"

"That depends on how I feel on the ride back into town."

Ivan got to his feet. Slocum searched him to see if he had a hideout weapon. He did not.

"Just sit there in the middle of the floor, Tolliver, and don't move."

"I won't move none," Tolliver said, and sat down, docile as a lamb.

Slocum walked over to look at Doc Leeds and Estelle. Leeds looked up at him and shook his head. Lurlene started to cry. Lenny also began to sob.

"I'm sorry," Slocum said to Lurlene. "I'm sorry it had to turn out like this."

Then he turned to Lenny. "Take Ivan into town and turn him over to the constable or whatever law you have there in Harrison. I'm leaving."

Lenny, stricken with grief, nodded.

"She's gone," Leeds said, and Estelle's three children broke down and began to wail and sob.

Slocum walked out of the Tolliver house and down the front steps to his horse. He climbed into the saddle and rode away, back toward town.

He wondered how he would explain all this to Linda Collins, and what would happen to her widowed sister, Meg.

It was really none of his concern now. He had done his job, and now all the skeletons in the Barneses' closet had been laid to rest.

He had horses to buy in Springfield, and maybe, by now, his big Palouse's leg had healed and the animal was ready to ride back to Kansas City as good as new.

He didn't hear Lurlene come out onto the porch and call out his name.

Slocum was already gone.

Watch for

SLOCUM AND THE GHOST RUSTLERS

283rd novel in the exciting SLOCUM series
from Jove

Coming in September!

LONGARM

**Explore the exciting Old West with one
of the men who made it wild!**